W
Lutz, Giles A.
Night of the cattlemen

5.95

	DATE DUE		XXX
MAR 2 1991			
OCT 6 1992			WITHDRAWN
MAR 1 1993			
JUN 1 9 2000			
AUG 1 1 '01			

Night of the Cattlemen

Night of the Cattlemen

GILES A. LUTZ

DOUBLEDAY & COMPANY, INC.

GARDEN CITY, NEW YORK

1976

All of the characters in this book are purely fictional,
and any resemblance to actual persons, living or dead,
is purely coincidental.

Library of Congress Cataloging in Publication Data

Lutz, Giles A
Night of the cattlemen.

I. Title.
PZ4.L976Ni [PS3562.U83]   813'.5'4
ISBN 0-385-12440-6
Library of Congress Catalog Card Number 76-22897

First Edition

CHAPTER ONE

Andy Brunner picked up a tin can, grunting from the twinge of pain the exertion caused him. He straightened without saying anything, but there was a tightness around his lips that spoke more eloquently than any words. He turned and faced Lige Madison. Brunner had once been tall, but age had whittled away at those inches, leaving him stooped. He was thin to the point of emaciation, and his leathery face was creased and lined. It was hard to tell his age; he could have been in his mid-sixties or mid-seventies. His hair was snow white, and his step wasn't as steady as it had once been, but those blue eyes were as bright and fierce as ever.

Lige didn't dare express the sympathy he felt for Andy. At the slightest sign of concern Brunner would jump down his throat. Lige knew Andy's rheumatism had a fierce grip on him this morning; it always did when the air got a little nippy.

Lige concentrated intently on the can Brunner held. He was partially crouched, his hand splayed, the fingertips almost brushing the butt of the holstered gun. Three months of this training were behind him. Several times he had regretted asking Andy to help him. Let him make a mistake, be a little slow, or thick-headed, and Brunner's tongue became a caustic whip.

Lige felt the strain of waiting creeping up his right arm. He dared not show his impatience, for Brunner would prolong the moment to test his alertness and concentration.

The old bastard, Lige thought with an inward chuckle. Brunner was really drawing him out this morning. Lige never moved his eyes from those twisted old claws about the

can. He had never quite come up to Brunner's harsh de-
mands, and this morning, he was determined he wouldn't
fail again.

Lige Madison was on the short side, barely topping five
feet six inches. His nineteen years rested easily on his face,
leaving it unmarked. His countenance was too sober for his
age, and the eyes too wary. He rarely smiled; when he did,
he showed strong, even teeth. His nose had a decided hump
in it, the result of a break healing improperly. He didn't
have much heft to go with his stature, and his lack of size
had earned him too many maulings from his two older,
bigger brothers. At least, he had thought of them as his
older brothers until three months ago. That was when he decided to ask Brunner for help. Those beatings from Hamp
and Ordie were going to stop.

The tension built up until it became painful. The itching
sweat popped out on Lige's forehead, and he wanted to
brush it away, but he wouldn't allow his attention to waver
in the slightest.

He caught the slight tightening of Brunner's crooked
fingers. Lige gripped the gun butt and drew in one single
fluid motion. He fired and hit the can just before it touched
the ground. Three additional shots kept the can bouncing
and skipping.

Lige straightened and grinned. He had a good grin, a
warm, infectious expression spreading over his face, giving
warmth to his usually sober countenance.

Brunner looked at his pupil for a long, appraising moment, then walked over and picked up the can. His expression didn't change as he examined the can, but Lige was
sure there was pleasure in Brunner's eyes.

Brunner limped over to Lige and held out the can. "First
time you ever hit it before it touched the ground. Four holes
in this can. At my best, I couldn't equal this."

Lige sighed. He had burned a lot of powder in achieving
this moment. "You think I've finally learned something,
Andy?" The grin completely changed his face. The cheek-

bones didn't look as sharp, and the lips fleshed out, taking away the thin, too intense look.

"You got a quick eye and a faster hand," Brunner said grudgingly. "I knew you had a special gift when I started working with you. At my top, I never went up against anybody as fast."

Lige felt warm and expansive under the praise. Years back Andy Brunner had the reputation of having the fastest gun in Wyoming. For twenty years, he carried a badge, and his gun kept a tight rein on lawlessness. He met all comers who tried to whittle on that reputation until finally people were convinced that to question Brunner's reputation was foolhardy. Crippling rheumatism accomplished what no gun could do. It was slower, though just as deadly as any gun Brunner ever faced.

Brunner reflectively rubbed the knuckles of his right hand.

Lige knew the hand was hurting again. "What's bothering you, Andy?" Lige asked quietly.

"I'm just wondering how wise I was in bringing out your natural gift, Lige," Brunner said honestly. "I guess it depends on how you intend to use it."

That cold, hard mask returned to Lige's face. "You needn't worry, Andy. I hope I never have to use it against anybody." He looked ten years older as he added, "Unless they force me."

"Anybody in mind, Lige?"

Lige debated a moment before he answered. Brunner had a right to know what was behind all his training. "Damn it, Andy. I'm sick and tired of Hamp and Ordie feeling they can knock me around any time they please."

"Thought that's what you had in mind," Brunner said carefully. "But it's a sorry thing when a man feels he needs a gun to go up against his own brothers." At the flare of temper in Lige's eyes, Brunner shrugged but plowed doggedly on. "I know what they've been doing to you. You could have stopped that abuse with a club."

"You think I haven't tried that?" Lige asked hotly.

"Whenever I did, both of them jumped me. A club wasn't enough to stop that. It only made the beatings worse."

Brunner stared stolidly ahead. For quite a while he had been aware of what was happening. Hamp and Ordie treated Lige as though he was a slave. They used a heavy hand whenever an order wasn't obeyed as promptly as they thought it should be.

"You could have gone to Travis," Brunner said.

"Travis knew what was going on," Lige said through tight lips. "He approved of everything Hamp and Ordie did. I've heard him say many times it was good for me. It might make me grow up to be a man."

Brunner nodded slowly. He didn't doubt what Lige said. "Travis is a hard man. I've wondered why his affection was for his two older sons with little left over for you."

Lige drew a deep breath. "Hold onto your hat, Andy," he said with grim humor. "Because this might knock it off your head. I'm not a Matlock. My real name is Madison. Travis isn't my father, and Hamp and Ordie aren't my brothers."

The shock of that made Brunner's eyes round with awe. "You're kidding," he said hoarsely.

"It's true, Andy. Don't look so upset. I'm damned glad it's true."

Brunner's bewilderment showed in his tone. "Then why in the hell did you stay around? Why, I'd think you would just pull out and leave."

"Don't you think I've tried that?" Lige asked harshly. "I tried three different times. Hamp and Ordie came after me. They worked me over pretty good before they dragged me back. The last time was the worst of all. That was three months ago."

"I remember," Brunner muttered. "You showed it."

"That's when Travis told me I wasn't a Matlock. My parents were Sarah and Bill Madison. They were killed in a stagecoach wreck when I was a year old. Millie Matlock insisted that she was going to raise her sister's baby. She took me in and raised me as her own." Lige tried to grin. "I guess that was one of the few times anybody stood up against Travis."

Millie's death was six years ago. Thinking about it still brought a lump into Lige's throat. Until three months ago, he had always considered her his own mother.

"When did you hear all this?" Brunner asked in a small voice.

"Travis told me the last time Hamp and Ordie brought me back. He went crazy when I told him I was going to leave again." Lige's face was frozen as he remembered that scene. The only solace he had was that Hamp and Ordie weren't around when Travis hit him with the news. If they had heard Travis, nothing would have stopped them from jumping him again.

There was pity in Brunner's glance. "Must've been a bad time," he said so low that Lige barely heard him.

"It was," Lige said grimly. "Travis raved like a madman. He said I wasn't of legal age yet, that I'd take his orders until I was." He grinned twistedly. "He spewed out how much I owed him for raising me. By God, I was going to pay some of that back. I was going to stay until he told me I could leave."

"So you listened to him," Brunner said, and there was new understanding in his tone.

"Until I can leave without worrying about Hamp and Ordie coming after me," Lige corrected. "That's why I asked for your help. I knew I was no match for them physically." Lige looked at the gun he still held before he slid it into his holster. "But this makes all the difference in the world."

Brunner looked at him. "I hope to God you're right." Of the three Matlock boys, he liked Lige the best. No, that was wrong, Brunner thought. Lige wasn't a Matlock. Travis was going at this all wrong, but Brunner still owed Travis a tremendous obligation.

"Lige, I felt guilty knowing Travis wouldn't approve of what I've been doing. Each time we sneaked out for another lesson, I held my breath, knowing how Travis would roar if he discovered us." He sucked in a deep breath before he went on. "When I finally took off my badge, Travis was the only one who tried to help me keep my self-respect."

Brunner's eyes were clouded with memory. The crippling rheumatism had grown worse, and the jobs he could find were few and far between. His savings were about gone when Travis gave him a job. "Lige, Travis kept me on long after my usefulness was gone. I can't forget that."

Lige could understand Brunner's feeling about Travis, but just the same he argued against his reasoning. "Andy, you don't owe Travis a damned thing. You saved his life. Cumshaw would have blown his head off if you hadn't stopped him." How well Lige remembered that day. He was only five years old, following Travis down the street, trying to keep up with his father's footsteps. He grimaced at the thought. Habit was a solidly rooted thing. Lige guessed he would refer to Travis for a long time as his father. Cumshaw had stepped out of a doorway with a shotgun in his hands, so drunk he was incoherent and staggering. Lige recalled how the blood drained out of Travis's face. Travis was unarmed and nothing he could say or do would have turned Cumshaw from his deadly purpose.

"You were there," Brunner said quietly. "Cumshaw would have killed him. I was across the street when it happened. I didn't want to kill Cumshaw, but I only had time for a snap shot."

"Did it really matter?" Lige couldn't keep the accusation out of his voice. "Cumshaw was only a sheepman, a sheepman Pa ran out of business."

Brunner's face burned a dull red. "Just a damned minute, Lige. You know I never took sides. I was only interested in saving a man's life."

Lige wanted to point out that Brunner had taken another man's life, but he held his tongue. Andy might claim he never took sides, but even while carrying a badge he showed where his sympathies lay. Brunner always thought like a cattleman. He had gone to work for one.

The anguish in Brunner's face softened Lige's mood. "Hell, Andy, I'm not accusing you of anything. You did

what you had to do. How did we get into this discussion? I
was only trying to make you see you don't owe Travis a
damned thing."

Brunner shook his head, a slow, dogged gesture. "I can't
help how I feel."

"Sure, you can't," Lige agreed. He threw an arm across
Brunner's shoulders. He knew a deep affection for this old
man. Ever since he had known him Brunner always had
time to stop and answer a kid's questions. Lige didn't know
of another man who would have spent so much time training him to handle a gun. Lige suspected Brunner now regretted giving him all these lessons. Brunner had polished
Lige's natural gift, knocking away the rough edges. More
than that, he had given Lige confidence. Lige now had the
means of stopping Hamp or Ordie the next time they made
a move at him.

Brunner scuffed at the ground with his boot. "When do
you plan on leaving, Lige?"

"Tonight, or tomorrow," Lige replied. "I've got to buy a
few new clothes in town. And I want to tell them I'm
going." He wondered how much false bravado there was in
his tone. "I can't just leave without telling them. That'd be
too much like running."

Brunner sighed. "I only hope you know what you're
doing."

"I do," Lige said crisply. "I made a promise to myself that
Hamp or Ordie were never going to lay a hand on me again.
Now, I can keep that promise. Damn it," he said heatedly at
the anguish remaining in Brunner's face, "can't you see what
I'm up against?"

Brunner sighed again. He saw it all right. But the three
Matlocks were hot-tempered men.

"I'm going into town, Andy. Anything I can bring you?"

Brunner shook his head. "Lige, I hope I haven't built up
any trouble for you."

"You've saved me trouble," Lige said. He knew he hadn't
gained an inch in height, but he felt two feet taller.
Confidence did that for a man.

"I can't teach you anything more," Brunner said wearily. "Just be smart how you use your new skill."

"I'll never be grateful enough to you, Andy."

"Sure," Brunner answered gruffly. He hesitated a moment. "All the luck in the world, Lige."

Lige lightly tapped the gun butt. "You've given me confidence, Andy. That's more important than luck."

them appear smaller, and now his scowl narrowed them until they almost disappeared. Livens did as little work as he could in running this stable; his increasing weight was ample evidence of that.

"The damned sheepmen are in town today," Livens growled and spat on the ground. "They just come in and take up space, getting in everybody's way. They sure as hell ain't buying anything. You ever hear of a sheepman who'd spend a dime, if he didn't have to?"

His own remark amused him, and he started to chuckle. He stopped, his eyes widening, and say, "Hey. You're wearing something new."

This was the first time Lige had worn a gun into town, and he felt self-conscious. "You mean this?" he asked, tapping the gun butt. "I thought maybe I'd run into a rattler on the way into town."

"Bull," Livens scoffed. "Too early for them to be out." He squinted at Lige. "You've got another reason. You have any trouble lately?"

"Who with?" Lige asked, trying to keep his face impassive. For a moment, he was startled into thinking that in some way Livens knew why he was wearing this gun. But that was impossible, he assured himself. Only Brunner knew, and Lige had never known him to be a loose-tongued man.

Lige realized what Livens was implying, and he shook his head. "If you aren't the most bloodthirsty man I ever knew, Sam. You'd like to see trouble break wide open, wouldn't you?"

"It's coming," Livens said belligerently. "Don't kid yourself it ain't. Hell, haven't you heard more flocks are coming into Wyoming every month. Those damned sheepherders are driving them in from California. Pretty soon there won't be a blade of grass that isn't covered with a woolly."

Lige grinned as he thought of all the acres in Wyoming. Livens' dire prophecy wouldn't come to pass for a long time, if ever.

"Laugh all you want to," Livens said stubbornly. "I'm tell-

CHAPTER TWO

Lander, Wyoming, was a thriving town. Last year had been a good year for livestock growers, and it showed in the town's air of prosperity. People were buying, and they thronged the stores. But it wasn't a happy town, for the air of tension was thicker than a dense fog. Lige could see it in the way people bunched up, avoiding other groups. He could easily pick out the sheepmen by their furtive manner and the wary look in their eyes. He wasn't a sheepman by any stretch of the imagination, but just the same he couldn't help but feel sorry for those harassed-looking men and their beaten-looking womenfolk. This was big country. There was enough land for everybody.

There hadn't been an open outbreak between sheepmen and cattlemen in the last few years, but Lige would bet that it was coming. As much dislike as there was between the two factions, it couldn't be bottled up long without an explosion. Lige was a cattleman, born and raised, but he still felt a strange sympathy for the sheepmen. That was a sentiment he kept to himself. Voicing it in a predominately cattle town would be worse than screaming heresy in church.

Lige rode into Livens' Livery Stable, and Sam Livens waddled out to greet him. Livens used to be a small cattleman, but he had never quite been able to make a go of it. He had traded his place for this stable. It looked as though he was making a living now, or at least, making more than he needed to eat well, for each time Lige saw him, Livens had picked up a few additional pounds.

"Hello, Sam," Lige said as he swung down. "Looks like the town is experiencing a good day of shopping."

Livens sniffed. The encroaching fat around his eyes made

ing you it's long past time for us to do something about those sheepmen."

Livens' heated words didn't erase Lige's amusement. "What are you doing about it, Sam?"

"Everything I can," Livens replied. "I've quit taking in a sheepman's horse. This stable is closed to them."

"Seems to me that's only cutting off your nose to spite your face," Lige commented. "You're losing money."

"Not much," Livens snorted. "How many sheepmen ride? They walk. At least, I'm keeping the smell of them out of my stable."

Lige didn't shake his head, though he wanted to. Blind hatred was a fearsome thing. It was a poisonous seed, and once planted, it grew and spread rapidly. Lige wondered how many people were thinking along the same line as Livens was.

"You'll see," Livens said heatedly. "One of these days, you're going to see the damnedest fight in the world. It should have been done before. The cattlemen may have waited too long. Putting off a job only makes it that much harder."

Lige wasn't going to stand here and argue this point with Livens, but just the same he knew a strain of worry. It wouldn't take much to stir up an already seething, bubbling pot.

"I'll worry about it when it comes, Sam," he said lightly.

Livens shook his head in reproof. "I thought you were smarter than that, Lige."

"Maybe I'll learn," Lige said flatly and handed his reins to Livens. "I'll be back in a few hours, Sam."

Livens wasn't through with his dire warning. "Lige, a piece of advice. If you're stopping in some place for a few drinks, stay out of Landerson's Saloon. That place is becoming a nest of sheepherders. If a cattleman wants trouble, all he has to do is go in there."

"I'll keep that in mind," Lige said gravely. He raised a finger to Livens and walked out onto the street. He wondered how much of this hotheaded talk was going around.

Until now, he had been too busy to hear any of it himself. An outbreak could happen, he admitted. Trouble between sheepmen and cattlemen was no new thing. It had existed for years, every now and then flaring into open violence. Lige would hate to see it happen again.

Lige pushed the disturbing thoughts out of his mind. Livens was just a big mouth, spouting off at the slightest opportunity. Livens couldn't do a lot of harm unless too many people listened to him.

Lige paused at the corner, debating what to do next. He had ridden into town to buy a new pair of pants, have his hair cut, have a few drinks, then enjoy a town meal.

It was early for the midday meal, but the thought of food won. Lige turned toward the best hotel in town. The last time he had eaten there, he had enjoyed one of the best meals he had ever known.

Lige walked the two blocks to the hotel. He acknowledged nods and greetings from friends and acquaintances. But several people, men and women, passed without the slightest indication of recognition. Lige couldn't detect any offensive smell from them, but he knew they were sheep people. Lige couldn't name all of them, but they knew him well enough. He could just imagine the mental curses thrown at one of those Matlocks. Lige got wry amusement as he thought he wasn't a Matlock, he was a Madison. He could just imagine the shocked surprise in people's faces if he attempted to make such an explanation.

He passed another stony-faced man and caught the quick, darting glance. Lige understood how a sheepman felt, but he still couldn't stop the wave of irritation their attitude aroused in him. If that was the way they wanted it, it suited him just fine.

He walked into the dining room of Wilkie's Hotel, and there were only two customers in the place. The lack of trade could mean the quality of Wilkie's meals had dropped. It didn't take long for such news to spread around. When that happened, business dropped off quick. No, Lige thought. He had been in here less than two months ago, and the food was excellent. It was early for the noon meal, and that was probably the reason for the lack of customers. The rush would start a little later.

Lige's eyes swept the room. The customer seated nearest him was a drummer. Lige had seen his kind before. Those flashy city clothes marked the man well. If a drummer ate here, it told Lige the food was still good.

Satisfied with his reasoning, Lige looked around the room. His face tightened as his eyes rested on Hamp Matlock.

Hamp's back was turned toward Lige, but there was no mistaking the awesome bulk of the man that just a short while ago he had called brother.

For an instant, Lige was tempted to turn and leave the room, then his jaw hardened. Damned if he would. Hamp's presence wasn't going to run him away from the prospects of a good meal. He didn't have to eat with him.

Lige crossed the room and selected a table as far away from Hamp as he could get.

Florrie appeared from the kitchen, carrying a glass of water. She set it before Lige, giving him a toothsome smile. She was a buxom woman, the fine lines of encroaching age beginning to crosshatch her face. But she was good-natured and liked to banter remarks with the customers. Rarely had Lige seen that good humor slip, though a few times he had seen the pleasant mask stripped away. He would say her feet hurt her then. A waitress's job must demand a lot of her feet.

"Hello, Florrie," Lige greeted her. "You got anything fit to eat in here?"

"You know better than that," she reproved him, but her eyes were twinkling. "What do you want us to do, spoil our record?"

Lige groaned in mock resignation. "I guess I'll just have to take what you bring me. I was thinking of a good steak." He indicated a measurement with thumb and forefinger. "'Bout that thick."

"I'll be right back and get the rest of your order," Florrie promised him. "I've got to get that drummer's order first. I've kept him waiting as long as I dare."

Lige's eyebrows rose at the asperity in her words.

Florrie's face flushed, and she said heatedly, "He's a pain in my—" She broke off the remark. "You know the rest of that. He thinks he's God's gift to all women. I can put him straight in a hurry. He's not any gift to this woman, not even an old, beat-up one like me."

Lige knew this drummer had been in here before. Florrie's dislike was too evident. "He's got a fat tongue, eh?" Beyond the remark, Lige didn't offer her any help. Florrie could take care of herself.

"And how," Florrie said waspishly and moved on to the drummer's table.

Lige watched with interest. The drummer reached for Florrie's hand, and she snatched it away before he touched her.

"It takes a lot of teaching to get anything through your head," Florrie said coldly. "All I want from you is your order."

Lige wanted to laugh at the red tide spreading across the drummer's face. Florrie had cut him down real good.

Lige didn't hear what the drummer ordered, but by the expression on Florrie's face she couldn't believe what she heard.

"You're kidding," she said incredulously.

Florrie's tone angered the drummer, and he became belligerent. "You advertise it," he said. "It's there on the wall. That's my order."

Florrie shrugged. "You've got to eat it, mister. Not me."

She moved to the service window opening into the kitchen. "Jim," she called. "The fancy dude wants a plate of sheep meat."

Lige didn't miss the contemptuous note in her voice. The order didn't offend him nearly as much as it did Florrie. He suspected the drummer had made his selection only to bait Florrie. Lige didn't care what the order was. The drummer had to pay for it, and he had to eat it.

The loud exchange of voices caught Hamp's attention, and he slewed about in his chair, turning a red, beefy face toward the drummer, then at Florrie. Lige thought, there's somebody whom the order could really offend.

Hamp's dull, porcine eyes came back to the drummer and remained on him speculatively. Lige suspected it would take a long moment before Hamp arrived at a decision. Hamp wasn't the fastest thinker in the world.

Hamp still hadn't noticed Lige, and again Lige was tempted to leave the dining room. The hell he would, he thought angrily. Too many times he had deliberately avoided Hamp. Lige was all through with that kind of running. Just the same he was grateful he wasn't involved in this little byplay.

Hamp's interest faded, for he turned back to his food.

Florrie came back to Lige's table, and twin spots of anger showed in her cheeks. "He does that to irritate me," she said angrily. "He ordered sheep meat when he was in here before, and I was just trying to be funny. I said I didn't know humans ate that. He's never forgotten it." She shook her head in an effort to throw off her anger. "Give me your order, Lige."

"A lot of people order sheep?" Lige asked curiously.

"Now and then," Florrie answered impatiently. "Wilkie insists on keeping it on the menu."

"It's his business," Lige said gently. "I guess a smart businessman reaches out for every dime he can."

"Meaning I should mind my own business," Florrie said. Her broad smile reappeared, wiping all resentment from her face. "You're right, Lige. Now, what do you want?"

Lige ordered his thick steak, fried potatoes, and a piece of apple pie. "That should hold me."

"You forgot coffee," Florrie reminded him.

"I sure did," Lige said. Despite her occasional resentment, Florrie was an asset to this business.

"Make that steak rare," Lige said as she started to move away.

Florrie turned her head over her shoulder. "Did you think I'd forgotten how you like your steak?"

Lige grinned. She had an awesome memory. Once she knew what a man liked, she never forgot.

Florrie walked up to the window and called in Lige's order.

Hamp turned again in his chair, looking directly at Lige. Well, Hamp knew Lige was here now. Lige half expected Hamp to rise and come over to his table, or order Lige to join him. Lige's jaw hardened. Hamp would be startled to find rejection for either of his proposals. Hamp might not know it, but Lige was all through taking orders of any kind from him.

The cook handed Florrie a plate. Lige knew his steak couldn't be ready this soon. That bowl had to be for the drummer.

Lige watched the drummer. If he didn't miss his guess, Florrie would slam the bowl down before him.

Hamp rose to his feet before Florrie reached the drummer's table.

Oh damn it, Lige thought. He's coming over here.

But Lige was wrong. Hamp wasn't coming his way. Hamp moved ponderously, his short neck wedged between those thick, bull-like shoulders. There was some mean purpose in those small, intent eyes. Surely, he doesn't intend to torment Florrie, Lige thought. A couple of times before, Lige had heard Hamp try to use his heavy-handed humor on Florrie. Hamp always came out second best.

Hamp intercepted Florrie's path and said, "Here, Florrie. Let me help you with that."

He took the bowl from her hand, turned, and stalked over to the drummer's table.

"Mister, are you the one who ordered sheep meat?" he asked.

The drummer looked up at him. "Why yes," he said. "I—"

Hamp didn't give him further time to speak. He upended the bowl and slid its greasy contents onto the drummer's head.

"I know nobody would order that to eat," Hamp said. His eyes danced with malice. "I figured you wanted to use it as a hair dressing."

The drummer sat transfixed in his chair, his face growing whiter. Gravy trickled down his face and stained his coat and shirt. He looked at his soiled clothing, then glared at Hamp. He pushed back his chair and sprang to his feet.

"What the hell do you think you're doing?" he roared. "Of all the clumsy clowns."

Hamp grinned at Florrie. "Would you listen to him? He's calling me names."

Florrie's eyes were dazed. "Hamp, why did you do that?" she cried. "Are you trying to get me fired?"

"Wouldn't have that for the world," Hamp replied. "I was just trying to teach him that ordering sheep meat isn't the smartest thing in this town." He shook his head in mock sorrow. "Sorta looks like he can't get anything through his head. Now, I have to do some mannering on him. I can't have him calling me names, can I?"

The drummer finally realized the menace in this hulking figure, for he retreated a step, his lips going thin and pinched, his hands held out before him.

"You keep away from me," he squalled.

Lige was pretty sure what Hamp intended to do. There was nothing Hamp loved more than beating on somebody with those massive hands. Lige thought it was time somebody stepped in and saved the drummer from a mauling.

"Hold it, Hamp," Lige called. "Right there."

Hamp's head swiveled toward Lige, and Lige saw a new purpose form in those dull eyes.

"Why, if it ain't my little brother," Hamp drawled. "Butting in where he's got no right to be. Looks like I'm going to have to do some mannering on him, too."

"Don't come any farther," Lige said steadily. He wasn't going to let Hamp get hold of him. Another step or two, and Lige would have to draw on him. He didn't think he would have to shoot Hamp. Just the sight of the gun should make Hamp change his mind.

"What's going on here?" an angry voice asked from the doorway.

Cass Duncan stood there. He was a solid, blocky figure of a man, and Lige couldn't remember ever seeing him angrier.

Hamp had respect for Duncan, for it showed in his changed tone. "Just a little fun with this drummer, Sheriff. No real harm done."

"Fun hell," the drummer screamed. "Look what he did to my clothes."

Duncan looked at the stained mess on the man's clothes. "This your idea of fun, Hamp? Maybe you'd better tell me all about it."

Hamp looked sullenly at the floor and didn't answer.

Duncan was losing his patience. He looked around at Lige. "What's your version?"

Lige's mouth tightened. He wasn't going to say anything to Duncan. It was up to Florrie or the drummer as to how far they wanted to carry this.

"Florrie?" Duncan said, his impatience growing.

Florrie gulped hard. She knew better than to try and cross Duncan. "Cass, Hamp dumped a bowl of lamb stew over this man's head."

Duncan turned toward Hamp. "Now, why would you do something like that?" he asked. His voice was deceptively soft.

"Aw, it just didn't seem right for him to be ordering sheep here," Hamp mumbled.

"Why?" Duncan snapped. "I always heard this was a free country. Suppose you tell me where I'm wrong."

Lige enjoyed seeing Hamp squirm. Words always hemmed Hamp in.

"Aw, Sheriff. You know how people feel about sheep around here."

"Some of them do," Duncan corrected. "You select yourself as a committee of one to change everybody to your way of thinking?"

Hamp flushed at the scathing rebuke. He pulled at his fingers, and Lige heard them pop. He wondered if Duncan was going to arrest Hamp. My God, how Travis would rant if that happened.

The same idea must have been in the drummer's mind, for he howled, "I want him arrested."

Duncan looked at the drummer with contempt. "What for? Did he hit you?"

"Look at my suit," the drummer yelped. "It's ruined."

"I don't think so," Duncan drawled. "Hamp, I figure you owe the man a dollar to get his suit cleaned, a dollar for his meal, and another dollar to Wilkie for necessary expenses in cleaning up this mess."

"Damned highway robbery," Hamp howled, but he was already pulling silver dollars from his pocket.

"Give the man two dollars and give the other one to Florrie." Duncan leveled a rigid finger at Hamp. "You're getting off easy. Another such stunt, and we'll see if some jail time will straighten you out."

Hamp was mad. Lige could see it seething in his eyes.

"Now get out of here," Duncan commanded. "Both of you Matlocks."

"Hold it, Cass," Lige said easily. "I didn't come in here with Hamp, and I'm not leaving with him, either. I just came in to have a steak. Florrie's already taken my order."

Duncan's eyes questioned Florrie, and she nodded. "All right," he conceded. "Stay and have your steak."

His eyes fastened on Lige's pistol. This wasn't the first time he had seen the gun, for Lige had noticed Duncan's eyes went to it when he entered the room.

"What the hell's that for?" he snapped. "You got ideas like Hamp? You looking for some sheepmen to express them on?"

Lige grinned. He wanted to say, God forbid, but he held the words. "If there's a law against wearing a gun, I haven't heard about it," he said easily.

"You just be damned careful how you use it," Duncan warned. "If you came into town looking for trouble, I can straighten you out, too."

Lige's grin didn't waver. Duncan was a good man to be

wearing a badge. He was hard and determined, adminis-
trating the law fairly, regardless of his personal opinions.

"You know better than that, Cass," Lige said.

All the suspicion hadn't left Duncan's eyes. "You just be
damned sure. Hamp, I told you to get out of here."

"I'm waiting for Lige," Hamp said stubbornly. His eyes
raked Lige. In the past, Lige would have quailed before that
look.

Lige shook his head. "I'm waiting for my steak."

"You heard him, Hamp," Duncan snapped. "Get out of
here."

Hamp tried to meet Duncan's probing gaze and failed. He
looked again at Lige, then turned and plodded out of the
room. That look promised Lige Hamp would have more to
say about this later.

"Everything settled here?" Duncan asked.

"It's not settled for me," the drummer howled. He looked
at the two dollars in his hand. "I've been cheated."

"My heart bleeds for you," Duncan said drily. He reached
out, took one of the dollars out of the drummer's hand, and
gave it to Florrie. He looked at her and asked, "Does this do
it?"

That gamin grin was back on her face. "Nicely, Cass."

"I didn't eat that food," the drummer shouted.

"You didn't pay for it, either," Duncan pointed out.
"Mister, I'd say you came out of this lucky. If you're real
smart, you'll just keep your mouth shut."

Duncan locked eyes with the drummer, and the drummer
gave way. He whipped around and stalked out of the room,
his muttering drifting back to them.

"I've run across him several times before," Duncan said.
"He's a damned nuisance."

Lige chuckled. "Florrie feels the same way."

"I know," Duncan said shortly. "Maybe I can have my
lunch in peace now. I'll eat with Lige. What did you say
he's having?"

Florrie repeated Lige's order, and Duncan blinked. "Too

rich for my blood," he said. "Only a cattleman can afford steak for lunch. Just bring me a beef sandwich."

Florrie nodded and walked to the service window.

Lige wondered what Duncan had in mind. Did he still believe Lige and Hamp were in this together and wanted to check further on Lige? Lige wanted to snort at how far wrong Duncan was in that speculation.

"I want to put you straight, Cass," Lige said as Duncan sat down. "Hamp was way out of line. He objected to the drummer ordering sheep meat. I avoid Hamp as much as I can," he finished in a flat tone. There was no need to give Duncan further explanation.

"Hamp is usually out of line," Duncan grunted. "The drummer's order didn't bother you?"

"It's his money. He can spend it any way he wants."

Duncan leaned forward, his face serious. "I'm glad to hear you say that. Hamp is typical of the hotheads in this country. If they can't find trouble, they'll make it. I feel like I'm sitting on a powder keg with the fuse already attached. A little incident like this could light that fuse and blow everything to hell. It was lucky this time it was only the drummer. He doesn't matter. If it had been a sheepman and he tried to do something about Hamp's handling—" He shuddered and didn't finish.

"I didn't know it'd gotten that bad," Lige commented. "But I don't keep up very well with what's going on. I haven't heard Travis say anything. He'd be the first one to rant and rave at the first incident."

"He wouldn't say anything to me," Duncan said gloomily. "I'm usually the last to hear anything about a new outbreak until it's exploding around my head."

Lige wouldn't have Duncan's job for all the money in the world. Duncan tried to walk in the middle of the road. That was a dangerous path, for he was liable to be hit by either side, or both at once.

"You've sure taken my appetite away," Lige observed.

"You're lucky," Duncan said sardonically. "You're only complaining about one meal. All of my meals are ruined."

CHAPTER THREE

As Lige stepped out of the hotel, the steak sat heavy on his stomach. He couldn't blame the cook for the loss of the steak's savor, and he couldn't blame Duncan for his gloomy words. Duncan had been through a sheep-cattle war before, and the memory had severely scarred him. Lige had no part in that outbreak, for he was only twelve. But Hamp and Ordie had been older, and Travis had taken them with him. How well Lige remembered his resentment at his father leaving him out.

Millie's words still rang in his ears. "It's not a game, Lige, something to look forward to. People will get hurt and die, and women will mourn." Lige could still see the stark tragedy in his mother's face. "Animals will be killed by the hundreds," his mother went on, "and all because men will not sit down and talk to each other."

"It's all the sheepherders' fault," Lige had said passionately.

Millie shook her head and said, "Lige, you're too young to see it any other way. How could you? Your father and brothers are cattlemen. When you get older, you'll be able to see that injustice can lie with the cattlemen as well as with the sheepmen."

Lige hadn't been convinced the night of that talk, but he had never forgotten his mother's words. He only knew there had been bloodshed in that clash, for he had seen women in black, their gaunt faces etched with the deep lines of their grief.

As Lige grew older he understood what his mother had tried to tell him. For the past several years, there had been an uneasy peace, but from what Duncan said, it was only a lull. No wonder Duncan was so worried.

Lige shook his head as he turned a corner. Would there ever be real peace in this country? There might be, if people's memories weren't so vindictive and so retentive, and if their damned tongues would stop stirring up the ashes of past clashes.

Lige snorted as he thought of Livens with his inflammatory remarks. Hamp was another one, eager to breathe life into coals that might die if he and people like Livens left those ashes alone. Yes, even the drummer had a minor part, ordering his sheep meat only as an annoyance to Florrie. The only wonder was that, with so many people blowing on those coals, they hadn't flamed into life before now.

Lige saw a man come out of Landerson's Saloon. He didn't know him and had no particular desire to, though something Livens said flashed through his mind. Landerson's was a nest of sheepherders, and by this man's dress, Lige would say he fitted into that category. The final, conclusive proof was that the man wore shoes. Sheepherders walked. Lige couldn't remember seeing one of them wear boots.

His head jerked up as three men stepped out of the alley that ran beside Landerson's. Lige had the positive feeling those three had been waiting for the man who had just stepped out of the saloon.

Lige knew those three men. They were riders for the Skull outfit. He had no particular liking for them, and it was probably because of the man they worked for. Harley Inman was an assertive, opinionated man, and his manner rasped Lige whenever he was near him. He was a lot like Travis. Lige couldn't help the comparison that flashed through his mind. The brand Inman used was a further affront to Lige. It was a grinning death's-head, bigger than a dinner plate. How many times had Lige heard Inman boast that anybody who fooled with any of his stock would wind up the same way as the brand he used, a skull. Lige never liked branding time at best. He saw no sense in inflicting unnecessary pain on a helpless animal.

Inman's three riders had the sheepherder boxed in, their faces set with some mean purpose. Lige was a good thirty yards from them, too far away to prevent an attack on the lone man.

"Hey," Lige yelled and broke into a run. Even if the three heard him, a yell wasn't going to stop whatever they had in mind.

The sheepherder tried to step around the three men blocking his path. Stobie Inman was the closest to the sheepherder. He was a younger replica of his father, with the same cocky, bragging attitude. Lige didn't like Stobie any better than he did his father.

Stobie grabbed the man's shoulder and swung him around. Haze Barnes stepped in and buried his fist into the lone man's belly. Lige heard his anguished grunt as the man doubled over, just as Wirt Thomas swung a clublike fist at the man's neck.

The sheepherder went down under the merciless battering, and he hardly hit the ground when Stobie kicked him. The other two joined in the savage kicking, and Lige was now close enough to see the wicked delight on their faces. Those three would kick the life out of the helpless man in a moment or two.

Lige's mouth was twisted with rage as he reached them, and his panting made his words jerky. "Goddamn it," he yelled, "that's enough." He grabbed Barnes by an arm and flung him around. He rammed his shoulder into Stobie's back, knocking him aside. Thomas stepped back before Lige could touch him.

"What are you trying to do, kill him?" Lige shouted.

That stopped the kicking, for the three whirled to face Lige. They were drunk; it shone in the gleam in their eyes, in the loose set of their mouths.

The momentary rage at Lige's interference washed from their faces, and Stobie spoke for them. "He's just a damned sheepherder," he said. His expression said he expected that statement to change Lige's attitude.

Lige glanced at the man. If he wasn't mistaken, this man

worked for Cleve Denvers. Lige searched for a name and came up with Pancho. If he had ever heard more, he couldn't remember it.

Pancho was doubled over on the ground, holding his abused belly, while he moaned softly. He wasn't unconscious, but he was hurt bad.

"So that was enough reason for you three to lay for him?" Lige snapped.

Stobie missed the blazing savagery in Lige's eyes. "Oh, we had another reason, though the first was enough. He's a damned Mex. He hasn't got any right to be working up here."

Lige quivered with rage at the blind cruelty of these men.

Before he could say anything, Thomas asked, "Do you know of any better reasons, Lige? Hell, we're not selfish. We'll let you in on the fun."

He started to turn back to Pancho, and Lige said harshly, "Your fun's all over. Let him alone."

The three exchanged astonished glances.

"Why, he means that," Stobie said in amazement. Outrage hardened his face. "If you feel so much sympathy for a damned Mex, maybe we can fix it for you to join him."

All three men were armed, and Lige crouched, his face turning cold. He had never drawn a gun on a man before, and the odds here were bad. But a display of resistance might change their minds.

Anger made Lige's voice shaky. "If you three are smart, you'll get out of here right now."

Again they exchanged mocking looks.

"Sounds like he's completely out of his head," Stobie remarked. "What are you going to do about it if we decide we don't want to go?"

"Then I'll have to change your minds," Lige said.

He had pushed this to the brink, and he doubted that any of them would take a backward step. Their pride, bolstered by their drinking, wouldn't permit that.

Thomas and Barnes started to speak, but Stobie stopped them. "I guess it's up to me to see what a damn fool he is."

Thomas and Barnes nodded and pulled away from Stobie. Stobie had a small reputation with a gun, and they were content to let him handle this.

"I guess he wants a hard lesson, Stobie," Thomas said and laughed.

"Any time you're ready, Stobie," Lige said calmly.

Stobie might be drunk, but not too drunk to know what he was doing. "You poor fool," he said pityingly.

Lige watched Stobie's hand. He saw the downward dip of the hand before he drew and fired. He hit Stobie before he could even touch his gun.

The bullet slammed Stobie out of his crouch, and he hung erect a moment, stunned surprise spreading across his face. His other hand half rose to a shattered shoulder, then he spun and fell.

"Jesus Christ," Thomas said in awed wonder. "He got Stobie before he could even touch his gun."

"By God, I can change that," Barnes said.

Lige's eyes blazed. "Try it," he invited. His tone begged Barnes to do just that.

Barnes looked at the pistol pointed at him and gulped. He had already seen evidence of superior speed, and the same gun was pointed at him. His mind wasn't too whiskey-fogged to ignore the unpalatable evidence.

Barnes licked his lips and carefully withdrew his hand from the proximity of his gun. "You picked the wrong man. You'll see," he said spitefully.

Before Lige could reply, he heard the noise of running feet coming from Landerson's door. A half-dozen men came pouring out.

What Duncan had been talking about in the dining room hit Lige suddenly. Now, Lige fully understood what Duncan meant. Lige hadn't picked a side; he stood squarely in the middle, and both sides would have liked nothing better than to squash him like an offensive bug.

"Hold it where you are," Lige yelled, halting the oncoming men. None of them was armed, and that was all to Lige's advantage.

The look on Lige's face, backed up by the drawn gun, checked them. One of them looked at the man writhing on the ground.

"What happened to Pancho?" he demanded. "Which one of you did it?"

"It doesn't matter. It's all over," Lige said. If he could keep them under control, he might be able to prevent this moment from exploding.

"The hell it is," the man yelled. His faced was twisted with raw passion. "Pancho wouldn't hurt a fly."

Lige felt the moment slipping away from him. There was too much hatred in these men. Words weren't going to faze them. In the next breath they would rush him. He was a cattleman, wasn't he? That automatically put Lige with the three who attacked Pancho. Lige could have pointed at the wounded Stobie on the ground, explaining his part in this, but he knew with a sinking feeling he would be wasting his breath.

Lige didn't take his attention from them, though he heard the hard pounding of feet coming down the street. He groaned inwardly. The gunshot had drawn more people. Lige could safely say that eight out of ten people in this town would lean to the cattleman's side. This could well break out into a pitched battle, and Lige was afraid he knew how that would turn out.

His face cleared as he heard Duncan's familiar voice.

"What the hell's going on here?" Duncan yelled wrathfully.

Some of the wracking tension left Lige. He was perfectly willing to turn this over to Duncan.

"Shut up," Duncan bawled as too many voices attempted to answer him. His hot eyes fastened on Lige. That was natural; Lige held the only gun in sight.

"You," Duncan barked at Lige, "start explaining."

"Stobie, Barnes, and Thomas were waiting outside here," Lige said carefully. "They jumped Pancho and knocked him down. They were kicking him to pieces when I arrived.

They didn't want to stop, and Stobie tried to back it up with a gun. I shot him."

Duncan looked at Lige for a long, sour moment. "You didn't lose any time using that thing, did you?" he asked bitterly.

Lige felt his face growing hot. "What did you expect me to do? Stobie drew on me first."

Duncan swung his head toward Barnes and Thomas. "That the way it happened?"

Barnes nodded reluctantly. "Lige beat him all right."

Thomas was still too drunk to be careful of his words. "Goddamn it, don't go trying to pin any blame on us. That damned Mex made a remark we couldn't take," he blurted out.

From Duncan's snort he must have known Pancho's inability to be aggressive. He looked at Lige. "That right?"

Lige shook his head. "I didn't see it that way. They jumped Pancho before he knew they were near."

Duncan eyed Lige thoughtfully. "Put that damned thing away," he said finally. He whirled on Thomas and Barnes, and his face blazed with indignation. "You drunken bastards. Get Stobie on his feet. All of you are under arrest."

"What for?" Barnes yelped. "By God, if you listen to that lying Matlock, you're out of your head."

Duncan's face was raw and violent. "I told you to get Stobie on his feet."

For an instant, Lige thought Thomas would still refuse, but Thomas wasn't that drunk. Thomas couldn't resist a last remark before he turned from Duncan though. "You just wait until Harley hears about this. He'll straighten you out in a hurry."

"Keep it up," Duncan said with ominous quietness. "I'll show you how fast I can break your head open."

Thomas didn't dare look at Duncan again. He and Barnes assisted Stobie to his feet. Stobie's head hung low, and he moaned, a soft blubbering sound. A spreading bloodstain widened on his right shoulder.

"How bad is he, Lige?" Duncan asked.

"I hit him in the shoulder," Lige replied. "You can see by the blood. I didn't try to kill him."

"Maybe it's too bad you didn't," Duncan muttered. "You know what those three will think of you."

"Remind me to worry about it later," Lige said.

Duncan shook his head. This wasn't the same Lige he had known before. He had seen the same thing happen many times. Let a man strap on a gun for the first time, and it seemed as though all his balances were distorted. He had some harsh words of advice to give Lige after those three were locked up.

Duncan spun to face the sheepmen. "What the hell are you standing here for?" he yelled furiously. "It's all over. Some of you pick Pancho up and do what you can for him."

Not a one of the six moved, and that enraged Duncan further. "Didn't you hear me?" His voice was crackling with anger. "I told you it's over. The three men who beat Pancho are arrested."

A thin slat of a man stepped forward. His hair was long, and he was heavily bearded. It was hard to tell the emotion on that face because of all the hair, but Lige decided by the raging eyes this man was mad.

"What will you do, Sheriff?" the man asked sarcastically. "Walk them down to the corner and turn them loose there?"

Lige expected to see Duncan explode. Nobody questioned his honesty or fairness without risking drastic retaliation. But Duncan's face showed nothing except that it seemed colder and harder. But his breathing might have been a little faster.

"You're Hammond, aren't you?" Duncan asked, running his words together. "Thank whatever god you pray to that I don't split your head wide open." His voice rose until he was roaring. "I said move. Now!"

That broke up all thoughts of further resistance. The men looked uneasily at each other, then helped Pancho to his feet. All of them turned and shuffled back into Landerson's. Their will couldn't stand up against the fury they saw in Duncan.

Duncan waited until the last one disappeared through the doorway, then said to Lige, "Let's go."

Lige's jaw sagged. "You're not arresting me?"

"Don't give me any back talk," Duncan said wearily. "Maybe you're the fuse I've been afraid of. Every place you go today trouble breaks out."

Lige wanted to yell at the unfairness of Duncan's accusation, but under Duncan's steely gaze he couldn't find the words.

"All right, Cass," Lige said, but he was shaking inwardly with justifiable anger.

Lige walked with Duncan behind the three men. He didn't say a word to Duncan until the three were inside the jail. Jesse Harper, Duncan's deputy was there, and his mouth dropped as he looked at the three men Duncan herded before him.

"What happened, Cass?" he asked.

"Lock them up, Jesse," Duncan said. "They just got so damned big they thought they could do anything they wanted."

Harper was a beanpole of a man with a long, horsy face. He had an annoying habit of sucking on his teeth whenever he was puzzled. He was doing it now. He rarely questioned Duncan's orders, but something was bothering him now.

"Cass, Inman won't be happy about this."

"You let me worry about that," Duncan said shortly.

Harper's face cleared. The sheriff was taking full responsibility and that lifted a load from Harper's shoulders.

"Come on, boys," Harper said, moving toward the cells.

Lige waited until the footsteps faded. "Aren't you going to lock me up too?"

"Keep on," Duncan said, "and I will. You sit down and keep your mouth shut."

Harper came back, and Duncan said, "Jesse. Go get Doc Daley. Stobie's shoulder needs looking after."

He waited until Harper left, then said quietly, "I thought I told you to sit down."

Lige was wise enough not to press Duncan further. The

sheriff was ready to explode. Lige sat down and stretched out his legs, feeling suddenly weary. He guessed emotions could wear out a man as readily as prolonged, hard work. Barnes' and Thomas's swearing drifted to him, intermingled with Stobie's groaning. Stobie couldn't help his moaning, but Barnes and Thomas better shut off that swearing before Duncan jumped all over them.

Duncan looked quizzically at Lige and remarked, "What got into you?"

Af first, Lige was going to answer that. If Duncan didn't have the story straight by now, he never would.

"Cass," Lige finally decided to say, "I never knew you to get things so mixed up."

Duncan rolled himself a cigarette and tossed the makings and papers toward Lige.

Lige caught them. Maybe he could take a little encouragement from Duncan's gesture. At least, Duncan wasn't so mad at Lige as to ignore the common amenities.

"I haven't got anything mixed up," Duncan said calmly.

Lige inhaled a long draught of smoke and blew it out as he stared at Duncan. If Duncan wasn't mixed up, then what was Lige doing here?

Lige tried to curb his rising temper. "What would you have done, if you'd come up on them?" he challenged.

"Probably the same thing as you did," Duncan acknowledged.

Now Lige was more puzzled than angered. "Then why did you bring me here?"

"You bother me," Duncan confessed. "This is the first time I've seen you wearing a gun. If you weren't looking for trouble, then why did you jump in on a sheepherder's side? You must be pretty good with that thing. I know Stobie has killed two men in gun fights, but from what I heard, you beat him easy enough."

Lige laughed wryly. "You've got it all wrong, Cass. I didn't stop to figure which side was which. All I saw was three men kicking another. Stobie wouldn't listen when I told him to stop. He drew on me."

Duncan still looked puzzled. Lige thought it wisest to explain a few things to Duncan now. "I'm wearing this gun, Cass, because Hamp and Ordie have knocked me around for too long. I just got tired of it," Lige said earnestly. "Travis wouldn't stop them, and I wasn't big enough to stop them unless I had some help. The gun is that help," he finished.

"Christ," Duncan said. "Your own brothers! You'd go that far to stop them?" he asked in awe.

Lige decided not to tell Duncan of the newly discovered relationship. He couldn't see where that was any of Duncan's business.

"I would," Lige said simply.

Duncan shook his head as though he couldn't believe what he'd just heard. "You just didn't pick up the ability to use a gun out of thin air. Somebody had to help you."

"Andy did," Lige confessed. "Every time Travis and Hamp and Ordie were gone, we practiced."

Duncan was big-eyed. "I'll say one thing. One of the best taught you. Didn't Andy object to your reason for wanting to learn to handle a gun?"

"I didn't tell him why I wanted to learn until this morning. I think Andy suspected something, so I told him. That rattled him pretty good. The lessons are over."

Duncan snapped his half-finished cigarette at the spittoon and missed. "I can imagine," he said drily. "I know how Andy feels toward Travis."

Before Lige could speak, Harper returned with Doc Daley. Daley was a stooped man with a gaunt, lined face. His steps were noticeably more infirm than they had been a few years ago.

"Jesse tells me you got a gunshot wound here," he said.

"Stobie Inman," Duncan replied. He offered no more information.

Those old eyes peered at Duncan, then at Lige. Daley's shaking head said this was bad.

"I'll look Stobie over," he said.

"You know the way, Jesse," Duncan said.

He waited until Harper and Daley left the room. "Doc

guesses you were behind this, Lige. It's going to cause a lot of talk around town."

Lige nodded. If Daley didn't spread it around, Harper would. He let the silence grow heavy between him and Duncan.

Daley was gone a good fifteen minutes. When he came back he said, "I see we've got a new gunslinger throwing his weight around town."

Lige's face reddened, but he let the remark pass. "How bad is he, Doc?" he asked.

"He's got a shattered shoulder, but the bullet went on through. He's going to be all right, but I doubt if that shoulder will ever be much good."

Lige kept his face stolid.

Daley was wound up, and he couldn't be stopped. "Damned if I don't hate a gun. I've seen too much of how a bullet can break a human body. Ought to outlaw the damned things," he finished grumbling.

That aroused Lige to indignation. "I suppose you think it would be better, if everything was left in bigger, physically stronger hands. That's what your way would do."

Daley blinked under the vehemence of Lige's reply. "That would be bad, too," he said in a milder tone. "Guess there's no solution to the problem."

He readjusted the angle of his hat and said briskly, "I'll be back to look at Stobie in the morning, Cass. He'll be here?"

"For quite a while," Duncan said grimly.

Daley walked out, and Harper started to sit down.

"Take another look around town, Jesse," Duncan ordered. "I want to be sure everything's all right."

He waited until Harper left, then looked at Lige with a touch of malice. "You didn't like what Doc said?"

"He doesn't know what he's talking about," Lige snapped.

"In a way, maybe Doc is partially right," Duncan said reflectively. "He sees only one side, the patching up, or the burying."

Lige was tired of Daley and Duncan jumping on him. "Can I go now?" he asked shortly.

"No." At the rush of blood into Lige's face, Duncan said mildly, "Damn it, Lige. This isn't any criticism of you shooting Stobie. But can't you see? It won't stop here. Inman's riders will do something about their feelings, and those sheepherders could be blaming you, too. I can control what Stobie and the others do for a while, because I know where they are. I can't do much about those sheepherders. They'll get together, drink a little more, and build up a mad at you. I want them to simmer down before you start out on the streets again."

Lige could see what Duncan meant, and his face cleared. "They won't push it any farther," he scoffed. "Hell, Pancho will tell them I was trying to save him."

"You hope he will," Duncan corrected. "But just the same, you're a cowman in their eyes. You're one of the same breed as those three are." Duncan jerked his head in the direction of the cell. "Time does more than anything I know of to cool down hot heads." He leaned back in his chair and stared at the ceiling. "I wonder how many men have died because of a so-called justifiable shooting?" he mused.

Lige nodded slowly. Every man had a different viewpoint, based on where he stood. Daley looked at it one way, seeing only human suffering. Duncan looked at an incident with a knowledge gained from experience that a shooting rarely just stopped there. He looked at the resentment and the hatings that sprang from that shooting.

Lige settled back in his chair. "I didn't have anything special to do, Cass. If it makes you feel better—" He broke off and grinned sardonically at Duncan.

"I can't do much about what happens out of town," Duncan said flatly. "But by God, I can sure do something about what happens in town."

CHAPTER FOUR

Lige looked at the clock on the wall. An hour had passed. "Can I go now, teacher?" he asked mockingly.

Duncan grinned. "I guess so. I hope you don't get your head blown off because I let you go too soon."

Lige chuckled. "You won't get an argument out of me on that."

Lige started to walk out, and Duncan stopped him. "Lige, you be damned careful how you use that thing you're carrying. Right now, I'll be damned if I don't agree with Doc."

"You mean outlaw guns, Cass? Sure would make your job easier, wouldn't it?"

"I'm not sure whether it'd help or hurt," Duncan said drily.

Lige laughed and stepped outside. He didn't expect any trouble, but just the same he kept his eyes open as he walked down the street. He had to admit Duncan's gloom had affected him. Duncan kept harping that one little incident could be the spark that set off the whole works. Lige swore at himself. Did he expect to see a bunch of sheepherders surround him with shotguns in their hands?

He shrugged and walked into Hinkley's Emporium. He was glad he didn't have to live around Duncan.

Clyde Hinkley hurried forward and greeted him. "How are you doing, Lige?"

"Good as could be expected," Lige replied. "I need a new pair of jeans."

Hinkley was a small, chubby man with a twinkle in his eyes. That twinkle warned Lige what was coming. The same thing had happened before.

"Got just your size," Hinkley said. He pulled a pair of

jeans from a stack and handed them to Lige. "How are these?"

Lige's face was impassive as he unfolded the jeans. He held them out before him and said, "I could make two pairs of these. They might fit Hamp. Not me."

Hinkley appreciated his own sense of humor. He chortled as he slapped his thigh. "By golly, they do look a little big, don't they?"

"Some," Lige said and grinned.

Hinkley refolded the jeans and placed them back on the table. He pawed through the stack, found another pair, and handed them to Lige. "These any better?"

Lige held them up. "These might come close to fitting. I need a couple of shirts."

Hinkley found the shirts and asked, "That all, Lige?" At Lige's nod, Hinkley said, "I'll wrap them for you, Lige." The memory of his own little joke was still with Hinkley, for he laughed as he wrapped the package. "Had you worried, didn't I, Lige?"

Lige was perfectly willing to let Hinkley have his fun. "You sure did," he said soberly.

Hinkley wrapped string around the package. "Bad, what happened a little while ago, wasn't it?"

"What was that?" Lige asked, keeping his face composed. Hinkley had probably heard about Stobie getting wounded. He wouldn't have the straight of the story. He hadn't been a witness. What he knew was handed him through a third or fourth party. Lige knew how inaccurate such accounts were.

"Those sheepherders jumping a bunch of cowboys. They laid in wait for them, then opened up from ambush." Hinkley breathed hard. "Those damned sheepherders shot one of the cowboys."

Lige curbed his impulse to put Hinkley straight. He doubted Hinkley would believe him. The incident made a much better story the way he told it.

"By God, it's got to be stopped," Hinkley said passionately as he handed the package to Lige. "Duncan doesn't seem to keep on top of the trouble."

Lige sighed. Here was another viewpoint, wrong as so many viewpoints were. Lige's lack of response seemed to prod Hinkley on. "I'm telling you a new war is about to break out. Somebody has to have a big foot to squash it before it spreads."

"You don't think Duncan has a big-enough foot?"

"Does it look like it?" Hinkley challenged.

Lige saw that he could stand here and argue with Hinkley for a solid hour without changing his mind, but he couldn't resist saying, "It looks as though you stand on the cattlemen's side."

Hinkley looked at Lige in astonishment. "That's a funny thing for you to say. Why shouldn't I lean that way? Do you know how much of my business comes from the cattlemen?"

"I guess that's a good enough reason," Lige said. He nodded to Hinkley and walked out of the store.

His face was thoughtful as he moved down the street. There wasn't much sane thinking in an age-old argument. It seemed as though a man instinctively picked his side without any effort to learn the truth behind the situation.

A small group of people was gathered before the stage depot, and Lige wondered what drew them. The stage had just pulled up, but a stage arrival was a common thing, by itself not enough to draw people's interest.

Lige quickened his pace. No, this was something out of the ordinary.

He pushed through the thin ring of watchers, and his face hardened as he saw Hamp. Apparently, Hamp was deviling a woman who had just stepped down from the stage.

Hamp's face was alight with wicked pleasure, and he said, "What's your hurry, honey? You shouldn't be in such a rush with all of your friends waiting to welcome you."

The woman's face was flushed with anger. "Get out of my way," she said contemptuously.

She had just stepped out of her girlhood days, Lige thought. She was a pretty little thing with her luxurious black hair framing her face and the perky little hat that sat on top of it. From here, Lige couldn't tell the color of her

eyes, but he could tell they were flashing with indignation.
Her face was as clean-cut as a cameo, and that well-formed
small jaw had a belligerent jut. Lige had the feeling he
should know her, but right now her name escaped him. No,
he thought, dismissing the feeling. He'd surely recognize
one as pretty as she was, if he had seen her before.

"Why sure, honey," Hamp said mockingly. "Anything you
say."

The small crowd was enjoying this, for Lige heard their
snickers and saw the smirks. His blood was boiling. He
didn't care who the woman was; there was no reason to
devil her in this manner.

The girl's glance was scathing, and her head was held
high as she started to step by Hamp.

"Aw, honey," Hamp said. His hand snaked out and caught
her arm. "Is this any way to treat an old friend?"

Lige was close enough to hear the enraged suck of her
breath.

"Let go of me," she snapped. Her anger ran her words together.

"Look at all that spirit," Hamp said. The crowd was
behind him, and he wasn't going to let this moment go.
"Ain't it a shame it's wasted on a sheepherder's woman?"

Lige shoved roughly at the two men blocking his way. He
parted them and stepped into the clear.

"Let go of her, Hamp," he said grimly.

It could have been the surprise of the order that made
Hamp release her arm. He whipped his head around and
mean satisfaction flooded his face.

"Well, look who's here," he said, his eyes narrowed. "If it
ain't Lige, trying to protect a sheepherder's woman."

Hamp still had the crowd behind him, for Lige felt the
weight of their silent censure.

The girl flashed a startled glance at Lige, then scurried
between the watching men. Lige was sorry he couldn't talk
to her, but that was impossible with Hamp here.

Hamp advanced toward Lige with heavy, ponderous
steps.

"Hold it right where you are, Hamp," Lige snapped.

Hamp's booming laugh rang out. "Listen to him. Sounds like he's grown up, doesn't it? Maybe I'd better show him his place."

"I mean it, Hamp." Lige couldn't help the tinge of desperation in his voice. He wasn't quite sure what he was going to do, but one thing was certain, he wasn't going to let Hamp lay hands on him.

Hamp kept up that slow advance, reveling in every step. He licked his lips, looked around at the crowd, and winked. "Talks big, doesn't he? We've got to show Lige how big he really is."

Hamp was less than two of those slow steps from Lige. It was either stop Hamp now or run. Lige was damned sure it wasn't going to be the latter.

He drew with a quick, flicking motion of his hand. "You always were thick-headed," Lige said savagely. "If telling you won't stop you, maybe this will."

Hamp stopped, his face going momentarily slack. "Would you look at that?" he said in wonder. "He really thinks he's grown up. I'll have to take that toy away from him, then give him a good beating."

Lige had been so sure he could face the moment of decision when it came. Now, he saw that he couldn't. He couldn't shoot Hamp no matter how much he disliked him.

But the hard core of determination hadn't dissolved within him. He wasn't going to stand here and take Hamp's promised beating before all these avid eyes.

Lige's throat was dry, and it took effort to force the words out. "I warned you, Hamp," he said hoarsely.

Hamp laughed again, a wicked burst of sound. He suddenly lunged at Lige, almost leaving his feet.

Lige stepped quickly to one side as one of those grasping hands brushed him. He raised the gun barrel, then crashed it down across Hamp's head in one sweeping motion.

Hamp plunged on but only for a short way. It looked as though his bones had melted. He fell on his face, tried to get his hands under him to lift himself, but they buckled. He went down again, and this time he didn't move.

"My God, did you see that?" one of the watching men asked. "Quicker than a snake."

"A damned rattlesnake," another answered him. "He hit his own brother."

Lige sucked in hard draughts of air. He looked at the crumpled form on the ground, awed by what he had done. He'd done exactly what he said he would. The way of accomplishing it was different, but that didn't matter.

He whipped around, his eyes hard and searching as they swept the crowd. He didn't know what they intended to do, but he wouldn't hesitate to prove how wrong they were no matter what they had in mind.

"Now what's going on?" Duncan asked. He sounded more weary than angry. He pushed through the onlookers and said flatly, "I thought I'd find you in the middle of this." He looked at the gun in Lige's hand, then his eyes went over Hamp. "So you did what you said you would," he commented.

Lige put the gun away. He felt like an egg-stealing hound, caught in the very action. "Cass, he was going to give me a beating." Lige gestured at the crowd. "All of them heard him."

"That so?" Duncan's cold eyes probed the onlookers, and several of them looked hastily away.

"Yes, he did," one of them muttered. "But Lige drew a gun on Hamp."

"Before or after Hamp's threat?" Duncan asked.

"I guess after," the speaker admitted. "But Lige had no right. He drew a gun on his own brother. Hamp couldn't stand for that, could he?"

"What happened?" Duncan demanded.

Lige answered that question. "He was molesting a woman who just stepped off the stage. I told him to let her go. He did, then turned on me."

"Ah," Duncan said tonelessly. He looked around. "Where is she?"

"She left," Lige explained. "I don't blame her. She'd been insulted enough."

Duncan's expression didn't change. "Who was she?"

Lige helplessly held up his hands. "I don't know. Though I felt like I should know her. Hamp called her a sheep-herder's woman."

"It was Lisa Denvers," a man in the crowd volunteered.

The name hit Lige hard. He knew a Lisa Denvers, but this couldn't be the same one. It had been a good four years since he had last seen the Lisa he knew, and there was no similarity between the two. The Lisa he knew had been all legs and arms, a gawky girl as awkward and uncoordinated as a newborn colt. The one he had just seen— He searched his mind for suitable phrases and gave up. This one was a woman.

"Ah," Duncan said again with no more tone than before. He moved to where Hamp lay and kneeled down beside him. Hamp had lost his hat, and Duncan bent closer to ex-amine the wound on his head. He looked up at Lige and said, "You must have hit him a good lick. Even with his hat on you split his head."

Lige looked down at the blood running down Hamp's cheek and pooling on the ground. He wasn't sorry. Hamp had kept pushing until he got what he deserved.

"That won't hurt him much," Lige said harshly. "He's too hardheaded."

Duncan stared at Lige before he straightened. There was some kind of a judging in his eyes, but Lige couldn't say what it was.

Duncan turned his head toward the watching men. "Some of you get Doc Daley. Hamp needs some patching up."

Those unreadable eyes came back to Lige, and he said, "You come with me."

"Not again," Lige yelped. "I told you he was bothering Lisa. What did you expect me to do?" Lige's tone grew more bitter. "Just stand here and take whatever Hamp wanted to dish out?" His passion grew until he was almost shouting. "Sure, I drew on him. I thought it would keep him off me.

But he just kept coming. Why, goddamn it," he raged, "I could have shot him. If you're going to arrest somebody, arrest Hamp. None of this would have happened if he hadn't started it."

"You coming?" Duncan asked. There was no giving in his voice.

Duncan waited until Lige fell in step with him. Nobody dared stand up before Duncan's hard eyes, and men parted to give the two passage.

"Teach him a good lesson," somebody shouted after Duncan and Lige.

"The damned fools," Duncan said bleakly. He didn't look at Lige nor speak to him until they entered Duncan's office.

"Sit down," he said.

Lige was boiling mad. "Aren't you wasting time? Go ahead and lock me up. I don't want to hear any lecture from you." This was proof of how wrong he was when he thought Duncan was a fair man. Hamp was the one who should have been arrested.

"Will you shut up?" Duncan shouted. His anger was greater than Lige's, and he outstared him.

He waited until Lige was seated, then shook his head. "I don't know what I'm going to do with you. You must carry a big paddle with you. Every place you went today, you've stirred up trouble."

Lige stared sullenly at the floor. Duncan was wrong again. Lige had had no intention of causing trouble anywhere he went. Things had just happened. Duncan certainly couldn't accuse him of making trouble when he went to Hinkley's.

Lige's head snapped up. He had forgotten all about his purchases from Hinkley. He didn't have the package now.

"Oh damn it," he yelled. At Duncan's surprised look, Lige said, "I bought some clothing from Hinkley. I dropped my package when I had that run-in with Hamp."

"You're lucky it didn't cost you more than that," Duncan said unfeelingly. "Don't argue with me," he roared. "Should

I have walked away and left you back there with them? You already had most of them against you."

Lige blinked. From Duncan's rationalizing it sounded as though he wasn't under arrest. He still burned at Duncan's handling of the situation.

"I could have taken care of myself," he stated. "I can't see where I did anything wrong."

Duncan slammed his fist on the desk. "Doesn't anything ever get through that thick head? If I was smart, I'd take that gun off of you and lock it up."

Lige glared at him. "You just try it." He was sorry the moment the words were out. He didn't want to set Duncan completely against him. "I'm sorry about that, Cass," he muttered.

Duncan shook his head. "Lige, you could be the spark I've been fearing. You could be the one spark that could ignite the town—maybe the whole countryside. You've sure got a start in that direction." He stared broodingly at Lige, then sighed. "You can't see that?"

Lige's jaw was a hard line. There was no use trying to make Duncan see reason.

"Didn't you know who that girl was?" Duncan asked.

"I remembered her when somebody said her name," Lige said in a low voice. "It's been a good four years since I last saw her." Lige thought of Lisa as she looked then and how she looked today. He grinned wryly. "She's sure changed."

"Is that all seeing her again means to you?" Duncan asked. At Lige's puzzled stare Duncan went on. "She's only the daughter of Cleve Denvers. That's all."

Lige hit his knee with his fist. Obviously Hamp knew Lisa and he figured anything he did to the daughter of a sheepman was justifiable.

Lige shook his head. If he had known who Lisa Denvers was before he acted, it wouldn't have made any difference. He would still have interfered.

"That still doesn't give Hamp the right to devil her," he said obstinately. He wondered where Lisa had been. Surely, he would have run across her before now, if she had been around.

"She looked like she was just coming back from a trip," he ventured.

Duncan nodded. "She was. She's been away to a school in the East. I'm surprised Cleve wasn't there to meet her."

Duncan made a tepee of his fingers and stared over them at Lige. "Now are you beginning to understand why that crowd was all for Hamp and against you? You jumped in on the sheep side and against your brother. By their standards, that was purely unnatural."

The anger faded from Lige's face and tone. "That still doesn't give Hamp the right to act like he did."

"It sure didn't," Duncan promptly agreed. "But do you think you or I could convince him of that?"

Lige considered the question for a moment. "The only one who can do that is Travis." He looked at Duncan and said softly, "It looks like I'm branding myself."

"Never saw a neater job," Duncan acknowledged. "First with Pancho and now with Hamp. I'm not saying you weren't right in both cases, but that won't gain you any favor. Don't you see, Lige? I have to hold you until I'm sure Hamp is gone."

"I appreciate that, Cass," Lige said simply. Hamp would never forgive him for busting his head. The next time Lige faced Hamp, he might have to do more than just split his head to protect himself.

The gloom didn't lift from Duncan's face, and Lige asked crossly, "Now what's wrong with you? I said I see what you're doing."

Duncan's sigh was a long, doleful sound. "You still can't see where you're headed, do you? It's not going to end here. What are you going to do now?"

"Why, I'm going home," Lige answered. He debated telling Duncan he wouldn't be there for long, then decided against it. That was still his personal business.

Duncan blew out a hard breath. "I thought you would.

Have you thought of what's ahead? You've got to face Travis. What then?"

Lige felt a tightness around his throat. Just the thought of what Duncan pointed out scared him.

"That's my baby, isn't it, Cass?"

"Yes," Duncan said gloomily. "I can't be with you."

"Who's asking you to be?" Lige flared. He stood and said, "I might as well be at it."

Duncan shook his head. "You're not leaving until I'm sure Hamp has ridden out of town." At the protest in Lige's face, Duncan said heatedly, "I might not be able to do anything about what happens at your pa's house, but I sure can do something about it here."

Lige nodded in understanding as he sat back down. Duncan was doing his desperate best to prevent animosity from breaking out into open warfare.

"How long are you going to hold me, Cass?"

"An hour. Maybe more. Until I'm sure Hamp is gone."

"My God, Cass," Lige said plaintively, "I can't spend the rest of my life sitting around in here."

"You may look back at this time and wish it had been a lot longer," Duncan said grimly.

Lige sighed. Duncan could be too close to the truth.

CHAPTER FIVE

At the end of an hour Duncan went out but returned shortly afterward.

"I just talked to Doc," he announced. "Hamp's gone. Doc saw him ride out. He had to put some stitches in Hamp's head. Doc said he was cussing his head off as he mounted."

"He would," Lige said shortly. He stood and stretched. Just this period of sitting had put a cramp in his muscles.

"Be seeing you, Cass," he said.

"Wish I could be of more help," Duncan said dully.

Lige could wish that too, but he said, "I appreciate what you did, Cass."

Duncan returned Lige's nod. Those worried eyes never left Lige as he stepped outside.

It would be dark in another hour, Lige thought as he walked down the street. That would be to his advantage. He'd just as soon not be riding home in broad daylight.

Lige passed several people on the street. None of them spoke to him, but he thought they gave him some strained glances. He didn't give a damn about what was on their minds. He was sure they knew what had happened. Nothing traveled faster than bad news in a small town.

Livens came out of his cubbyhole to meet Lige as he walked into the runway.

"Get my horse, Sam," Lige said.

"You sure asked for it, didn't you?" Livens asked.

For a moment, Lige didn't know what he meant, then it came to him. So Livens had heard about his tangling with Hamp, and not favorably, Lige thought in resignation. He didn't want to hear any more about it from Livens, and he said crossly, "Just keep your mouth shut, Sam."

Livens looked aggrieved, but he didn't comment further.

Lige heard him muttering to himself as he walked away shaking his head. There wasn't a sympathetic ear in the whole damned town except Duncan's.

Lige paid Livens when he returned with his horse and mounted. He almost chuckled as he thought, after today Livens wouldn't want his business any more, either.

It was dark when Lige arrived home. He rode into the barn, and Brunner was there.

The look on Brunner's face told Lige that Brunner knew, too.

"So you've heard about it?" Lige said bleakly.

"How could I help it?" Brunner replied. "Hamp rode in with his head bandaged. I got a good cussing out when I asked what had happened."

"Did he tell you, Andy?" Lige asked woodenly.

"From what I could pick out between swear words, you jumped him for no reason at all. He was merely joshing a sheepherder's woman, and it upset you. Is that the way it happened, Lige?"

"Not quite," Lige answered. "He was manhandling Lisa Denvers. When I told him to stop, he turned on me. I drew on him, thinking it would put some sense in his head, but Hamp was playing up to a watching crowd. He told the crowd he'd take the gun away from me and give me the beating I deserved. I couldn't shoot him, Andy. But by God, I didn't hesitate to bust his head open."

"Oh Jesus," Brunner moaned. "Cleve Denvers' daughter. Cleve won't forget that. And Hamp won't forgive what you did to him."

"You can add Travis to your list," Lige said. "Could I have done anything else, Andy?"

Brunner thought for a moment before he shook his head. "I don't see how you could. Oh damn," he said sorrowfully, "I'm sorry I ever taught you to use that gun."

Lige remembered his savage pleasure as he struck Hamp down. "I'm not," he said hotly. "You'd rather see Hamp or Ordie knock me around?"

Brunner shook his head. "You know I don't want that. But what are you going to do now?"

Lige shrugged. "Go in and face them and get it over with."

"Do you want me to go with you, Lige?"

Brunner was offering the only thing he had; his job. Just one word in defense of Lige, and Travis would fire him. "No, Andy," Lige said gently. "It wouldn't change anything."

"I guess not," Brunner muttered. He was obviously distressed.

"Just hold my horse for me," Lige said. "I might be needing him sooner than I expect."

Lige walked toward the house. With each stride that familiar scared feeling was growing steadily.

He looked in the kitchen window before he moved to the door. Travis, Hamp, and Ordie were all there. Lige sighed. He might as well face all three of them at once and get it over.

Lige stayed there a moment, looking at them. Hamp's head was bandaged, and as Lige watched, Hamp poured himself another drink. By the flush in Hamp's face, he had been drinking ever since he arrived.

Lige's eyes switched to Ordie. Ordie was a year older than Hamp, and he had a striking resemblance to his brother; the same awesome bulk, the same heavy face.

Lige looked at Travis. Both of Travis's sons looked like Travis, Lige thought, except that with his years Travis had picked up a lot of weight. His normal speaking voice was a roar. Travis was furious. It showed in the heavy color in his face, the way he paced back and forth. Every now and then, he paused to stab a finger at Hamp or Ordie.

He's really mad, Lige thought dismally. He couldn't remember seeing Travis more furious. He had always been more fearful of Travis than of Hamp or Ordie. All Lige had ever known from Travis was a shouted order, and a quick, heavy, backhanded slap when Lige didn't obey fast enough to suit him.

I wonder how Millie ever stood him, Lige thought as he turned toward the door.

Lige hesitated with his hand on the knob. He felt cold all over, even though he was sweating. The longer you stand out here, the more you weaken, he told himself.

He turned the knob and swung the door wide. His face was as white as a granite slab.

"Hello, Travis," he said and cursed himself for the squeakiness of his voice.

Travis whirled to face him, looking stupefied at Lige's appearance.

"I'll be goddamned," he said thickly. "I didn't think you had the guts to show up here again." Lige's audacity choked him, and when Travis tried to say something else, he spluttered.

"Don't be mad at him, Pa," Hamp said, grinning widely. "Lige knew we'd be worried about him."

Ordie just sat and grinned at Lige. It was an evil grin, promising unspeakable things.

Lige swallowed to keep his voice steady. "I guess you heard about it."

The rush of blood turned Travis's face purple. "You're goddamned right I have," he roared. He spat on the floor in disgust. "Pulling your gun on Hamp and hitting him with it just because of a sheepherder's woman."

"Did he tell you what he was doing?" Lige asked. The tremor in his voice threatened to betray him. "He was manhandling a woman in public. I knew you wouldn't want that." Lige rushed on, trying to build up conviction in his voice. "I told him to stop, but he wouldn't listen. That's when I drew on him. Even that didn't stop him."

"So you stopped him," he said with ominous quietness.

Lige felt helpless and hemmed in. "I did. I wasn't going to stand there and let him maul me before all those people." The look on Travis's face told Lige he wasn't gaining ground.

"You didn't know who the woman was?" Travis asked.

"I heard later," Lige admitted.

"Cleve Denvers' daughter." Travis sounded as though he had something foul in his mouth. "And you stand up for trash like that."

Lige's mouth tightened. He remembered how Lisa Denvers looked, the proud cant of her head, the line of her nose and chin.

"You've got no right to say that," Lige objected.

It would have been far more natural if Travis raved and ranted, but the disturbing quietness remained in his voice. "If you'd known who she was, would you still have hit Hamp?"

A lie might give Lige his escape, or at least lessen Travis's wrath. "I would have," Lige said stubbornly.

Travis's breathing had a queer, rasping sound. "Listen to that," he roared. "It's pretty plain he'd pick a damned sheepherder against his own kind."

It surprised Lige to realize the inner shaking had stopped. Now, he was just mad. "I would have done the same, regardless of what woman was involved."

"Listen to that, boys," Travis finally managed to say. "Lige hasn't learned very much, has he? Looks like our teaching has been on the short side. Maybe you two better remedy that right now."

Ordie's grin split his face from ear to ear as he pushed to his feet. Hamp had the same assured smirk.

"Pa," Hamp said with mock gravity, "Lige is going to thank us for the good we'll do him."

They split, coming at Lige from different angles.

Lige had two courses; he could stand here and take the punishment they intended giving him, or he could bolt out of the door.

Lige didn't give either course any consideration. "Better call them off, Travis." His face was pale and tight, but there was no quaver in his voice.

"Ain't going to do you any good to beg," Travis said. "After this is over, maybe you'll start thinking straight."

Ordie and Hamp thought they were tormenting Lige, for

they took mincing steps at him instead of making a concentrated rush.

"If you won't stop them, Travis, I will." Lige drew before the echo of his words faded.

Travis blinked in surprise at Lige's speed, but he was a hardheaded man. Once an idea was lodged in his head, it was almost impossible to dislodge it.

"Would you look at that?" Travis asked. "Real slick with that thing, ain't he? He drew on us." His face turned ugly, and his eyes were hot coals. "He's gonna be real hard to convince, boys."

The sight of the gun momentarily stopped Hamp and Ordie. Hamp licked his lips, as though uncertain about a course of action. Lige thought Hamp could be recalling a similar encounter. He hoped so. Hamp had gotten a broken head out of that one.

"He won't shoot us," Hamp said with a new-found conviction. "He might knock one of us down. But he can't get us both at the same time. One of us will get him. Come on, Ordie." He started that slow, ominous advance again.

"I told you," Lige said in a steady voice. He fired, and the bullet gouged a long splinter from the floor, nipping at the edge of Hamp's boot sole. The shot was close enough to put a tingling in Hamp's foot, for he danced on one foot while holding the other.

"You shot me," he howled.

"I could have," Lige corrected. "The next one will be through your foot."

Ordie turned a scared face toward Travis. "Pa, he means it. He's gone clear out of his head."

All three of them were shocked into inaction. Hamp forgot about his foot. Ordie's eyes were wide with apprehension, and Travis was stunned.

Lige took advantage of the moment to try to talk some sense into Travis's head. "Travis, you sicked them on me. I don't want to have to shoot either of them. But Ordie and Hamp aren't going to knock me around any more."

Travis spit all over his chin, and he looked as though he

was choking on his tongue. "Why damn you," he finally managed to get out. "You put that gun away. Right now! You hear me?"

"Travis, you know better than that," Lige said calmly. "I only came back to tell all of you that I'm leaving. For good. I'll shoot the first one who tries to stop me."

Travis's face was an apoplectic hue. "You ain't going anywhere unless I tell you."

Lige shook his head in pitying disbelief. "Travis, you order those two around from now on. They have to take your orders. I don't any more."

Hamp and Ordie were shocked by Lige's rebellion. Evidently Travis hadn't told them about Lige not being a Matlock.

"Travis, you did me a big favor when you told me I didn't belong to you," Lige said. "It makes me feel like I've just had a bath I've needed for a long time."

Hamp looked from Travis to Lige. "What's he talking about?"

"Hasn't he told you and Ordie yet?" Lige asked derisively. "I'm not your brother and never have been. You try again to drag me back, and I'll blow your head off."

The shock of those words loosened Hamp's mouth. "Is he telling the truth, Pa?"

Travis was furious that the subject came up at all. "He is," he admitted. "He never belonged to me. I raised him because Millie insisted. The best you can call him is a cousin. But he ain't going until I tell him he can. He's not legal age yet. I spent a lot of money raising him. I'm going to work some of that money out of him."

A new savagery came into Hamp's eyes as he looked at Lige. "I never did have much use for you. This is going to make it a lot easier. We don't have to handle him with gloves any more. He ain't going any place until you say the word, Pa."

"You'd better call them off, Travis," Lige warned again.

"Don't let him mouth off like that," Travis screamed. "What are you standing there for? Rush him."

Ordie licked his lips. "He means it, Pa," Ordie mumbled. "We ain't armed. He'd shoot us down before we reached him."

If Travis heard Ordie, he didn't show it. "Rush him," he screamed. "Rush him."

Lige fired another bullet into the floor between Ordie's feet to strengthen his wavering decision.

Ordie backed away, his eyes rolling. "Not me, Pa. Not against that crazy man."

Hamp showed no more inclination than Ordie to obey Travis. "Not me, Pa," he said, shaking his head. "We'll find a better time."

Travis was wild with rage. "Get out of here," he screamed at Lige. "Get out of my house."

"I'm going." Lige almost said "Pa" and caught himself just in time. He didn't have a stomach any more. All he had was a churning, empty mass where his stomach should be.

Lige backed out of the door. He could still hear Travis raving. The three of them started to crowd through the door after him. He fired over their heads, hearing the slam of the slug into wood. They ducked out of sight, but that shot wouldn't hold them long. Lige knew they would be grabbing for their guns.

Lige whirled and ran toward the barn. Brunner stood in the doorway, holding the reins of Lige's horse.

"What was all that shooting about?" Brunner asked worriedly.

"No time to explain now, Andy," Lige replied. "Just a disagreement." He smiled bleakly at the understatement. "I didn't shoot any of them." He vaulted into the saddle and paused long enough to say, "Stay out of this, Andy. Don't let them know you're involved in any way."

Brunner understood what Lige meant. He shook his head, then turned and ran into the barn. Lige heard the fading sound of his pounding feet. Brunner was hurrying toward the rear door of the barn. He was smart enough to stay out of sight until things quieted down.

Lige spun the horse and set it into a hard run. He heard

the long, whipping echo of a rifle bullet and crouched low in the saddle. He bent lower as several shots searched for him. He had one small consolation. It was dark, and enraged men didn't shoot very well.

He straightened after a couple of hundred yards. He could still hear the rifle shots. Those three were sure wasting a lot of ammunition.

CHAPTER SIX

Hamp poured himself another drink before he said, "Better stop that pacing, Pa, before you wear yourself out."

Travis paused long enough to give him a bitter glance. "You two let me down. You just stood there and let Lige walk out untouched."

Ordie flushed at the implication. "You calling us yellow, Pa?"

"Can you call it anything else?" Travis yelled. "If the two of you had rushed him together, you'd have swamped him under before he could shoot."

Hamp drained his glass and looked judiciously at Travis. "We'd have swamped him with our dead bodies, Pa. My God, did you ever see anyone as fast? He don't shoot so bad, either. For a few seconds, I thought he'd blown my foot off. I've got the feeling he could just as easily have put a bullet anywhere he wanted." He stared reflectively at the few remaining drops in his glass. "I found out one thing. I sure don't want to face him with a gun in his hand."

Travis's mouth opened, and Hamp said in a firm voice, "Don't go calling us yellow again, Pa. You weren't any more eager to get at him than we were."

Travis tried to outstare Hamp and failed. His whole world was falling down around his head. First, Lige had dared to stand up against him, and now Hamp and Ordie were doing the same thing.

Travis sank into a chair and glared bitterly at his sons. "My God, what have I raised?"

Hamp considered the question. "If you don't know, Pa, we sure don't. We thought Lige belonged to you. Was what you said to him true?"

"It's true," Travis said heavily. "Both of you were too young to remember. I took him because Millie insisted." He stared at the floor. "I thought I could raise Lige into something. I sure as hell failed."

"I wouldn't say that, Pa," Hamp said and grinned. "He sure turned out to be a gunslick. Where did he learn to handle a gun like that?"

"I don't know, and I don't give a damn," Travis said hollowly. "I never want to set eyes on him again."

"I do," Hamp said positively. "I've got a big score to settle with him."

"Me too," Ordie echoed.

Hamp grinned. "Looks like Ordie feels the same way. We'll run across him again."

"You won't," Travis flared. "You saw the way he took out of here. He won't stop until he runs into the ocean."

"I don't know, Pa," Hamp said thoughtfully. "I've got a funny feeling we'll see him again." He closed his hand, turning it into an awesome ham-sized fist. "That'll be the day," he said savagely. He turned his head toward the door. "Did I hear a horse come up?"

"I heard it too," Ordie exclaimed.

Travis must have heard it also, for his eyes filled with a wicked gleam. "Maybe after Lige got a short distance away, he realized what he was throwing away. Maybe that's him coming back to beg me to forgive him."

Hamp shook his head. "Naw, Pa. I don't think so. Lige wouldn't be that crazy."

Hamp stood at the hard pounding on the door. "Whoever it is sounds like he's trying to beat the door down," he grumbled. "Still think it's Lige, Pa?" he asked sardonically.

"See who it is," Travis snapped.

Before Hamp reached the door, the pounding came again. "Travis," a furious voice yelled, "are you in there?"

"Sounds like Inman to me," Hamp said as he took hold of the knob. "Something's really got him upset."

He opened the door and whistled at the blazing anger on

Inman's face. "What's eating on you, Harley?" Hamp stepped aside and said, "Come in, come in."

Inman stalked into the room with stiff-legged steps that drove his boot heels hard against the floor. He stopped before Travis and yelled, "I want to see Lige. Right now!" His ordinarily florid face was far redder than usual.

Travis bristled at Inman's tone and attitude. "Don't talk to me like that," he said, his voice edged. "Who in the hell do you think you are to come busting in here and demanding things?"

Inman made a quick survey of Travis's face and cooled down. "I didn't mean to come on so strong, Travis," he apologized. "But I want to see Lige."

"Harley, you missed him by about twenty minutes. He tore out of here like his tail was on fire."

Harley Inman swore helplessly, got control of himself, and asked in a calmer voice, "When do you expect him back, Travis?"

"Never, for all I care," Travis said grimly. "I threw him out for good."

Inman beat his hands together in frustration. "Damn it! I got something to settle with him."

"What did he do to you?" Hamp asked curiously.

"He shot Stobie in the shoulder," Inman raged.

That startled Travis and left him groping for words. "In a fair fight?"

"Duncan said it was," Inman replied. "Though I have my doubts. Stobie is a pretty fair hand with a gun."

"We found out Lige is pretty good, too," Hamp said. At Travis's withering glance he fell silent.

"What happened, Harley?" Travis asked.

"Stobie, Barnes, and Thomas were in town," Inman answered. "They passed a sheepherder on the street. Stobie thought he's called Pancho. Do you know him?"

"Doesn't he work for Denvers?" Travis asked.

Inman nodded. "Pancho said something offensive to Stobie and the boys, something they couldn't let go by." He saw the bottle, sitting on the table and asked, "Can I have a drink? I need it to settle down."

Hamp shoved his glass forward. "Help yourself."

Inman half filled the glass and downed it. "Ah," he said as he wiped his lips with the back of his hand. "I sure needed that."

"Go on," Travis said impatiently. "Tell me what happened."

"The boys were giving that sheepherder the beating he needed when Lige stopped them. Lige drew on Stobie before Stobie realized what was happening."

Hamp shook his head. He had seen two examples of Lige's speed. He didn't think Stobie Inman could compare with Lige.

"You don't believe that?" Inman demanded.

Hamp shrugged. "I don't know. I wasn't there."

"Harley, will you get on with it?" Travis yelled.

"Duncan came along then. He arrested my boys for causing all the trouble." Inman beat a fist into a palm. "Why damn it, Lige did all the shooting, but Duncan didn't arrest him."

Hamp had enough liquor to make his tongue unruly. He didn't care what Travis or Inman thought; he was going to say what was on his mind. "Maybe Duncan had a reason," he grunted. "From what I heard, it sounds like Stobie tried to pull on Lige and couldn't make it." At the rage in Inman's face, he said defiantly, "I've seen Lige in action twice. I don't think Stobie ever saw the day he could beat him."

Travis sounded as though he was choking, and Inman's breathing made a queer, whistling sound. Now, Hamp had both of them on his back, but he went ahead doggedly. "I ain't trying to rile you, Harley. But I think you're lucky you didn't find Lige here. Particularly, if you came here to call him on this."

"I think you'd better explain that," Inman said. The words sounded as though they were honed on the edges of his teeth.

"Lige's pulled a gun on me twice. The second time was

just a few minutes ago." Hamp sucked in a ragged breath. He didn't care how angry this made Inman, or how much humiliation Travis might feel. He touched the bandage on his head. "If you're wondering about this, I got it from trying to stop Lige in town. I was going to give him a good beating there, but he drew on me. He's never stood up to me before," Hamp said reflectively. "I thought I could take that gun away from him." He spread his hands and said simply, "I couldn't. He busted me with the gun barrel."

"What the hell's been going on here?" Inman exploded.

Hamp didn't dare look at Travis. He was in this far, and he couldn't back out.

"Lige came home, and Travis wanted Ordie and me to knock some sense into him." Hamp shrugged. "We couldn't." He pointed at the bullet gouge in the floor. "Lige drew on us and warned us to stay away. When we kept coming at him, he fired. For a minute, I thought he took my foot off. His bullet nipped my boot sole." Hamp shook his head in wonder. "I never saw anybody faster, and I've seen Stobie's speed." He grinned sheepishly. "Ordie and me decided we wanted no part of Lige."

"It was a family argument," Travis said hastily before Inman could pry further. His look warned Hamp to say nothing more about it.

Inman looked from Travis to Hamp. "Why did Lige draw on you in town?" he asked bluntly.

"Aw," Hamp said and stopped. He wished he could back out, but he knew better than that. Inman wasn't a man who took kindly to having his questions ignored.

Hamp popped a knuckle before he said, "I was just having fun with Lisa Denvers. She'd just stepped down from the stage. Lige didn't like what I was doing."

"I'll be goddamned," Inman said. "Cleve Denvers' daughter?"

"Yeah," Hamp acknowledged without looking at Inman.

Inman stared at Travis, and his expression was calculating. "It's damned funny, Travis. First, Lige interferes with my boys over Pancho, then he butts in again because of Lisa Denvers. Do you know what I think, Travis?"

"No," Travis said sullenly.

"Travis, it looks to me like you raised a sheepherder instead of a cowman."

That purplish hue filled Travis's face again, showing how raw Inman's remark raked him. "That's enough, Harley," he thundered. "Don't say any more. I threw Lige out for good. He'll never come back here again."

Inman shrewdly eyed Travis. "Are you going to sit here and do nothing, Travis?" he asked softly. "Lige's rubbed your nose into the dirt pretty good." He raised a hand to check Travis's outburst. "I know. You can't get your hands on him now."

"Leave it alone," Travis warned.

Inman grinned bleakly. "I don't know what happened here, Travis, and that's your business. But I never figured you'd be the man to take abuse without raising a hand."

Travis glared suspiciously at Inman. "What are you trying to say?"

"You've got a lot of insults to wipe out, Travis," Inman said smoothly. "So have I. Doc Daley told me Stobie's shoulder wouldn't ever be any good again. It looks like both of us have lost sons."

Hamp watched his father covertly. At any moment, he expected to see Travis charge out of that chair and throw Inman out.

"You'd better say it plainer," Travis said with ominous quietness.

"It looks to me like there's only one man behind all our trouble. Cleve Denvers! Goddamn it, how much longer are we going to take the crap the sheepmen hand us?"

Some of the angry color was fading from Travis's face. "What are you driving at?" he growled.

"I say it's time we band together and drive the damned sheepmen out of the country."

"Duncan won't stand for that," Hamp bleated.

Inman sneered at him. "Travis, don't tell me you've raised another spineless son."

"Shut your mouth," Travis roared at Hamp. "Go get a fresh bottle. We've got some talking to do."

CHAPTER SEVEN

Lige hadn't the slightest idea where he was going, though he no longer felt the need to hurry. For the first mile or so, he kept glancing over his shoulder, fearing pursuit. Now, he could relax. Travis and Hamp and Ordie hadn't set out after him, or else he had lost them. Lige hoped he would never see any of them again. He could say that honestly, without a semblance of spite or retaliation. He knew if he faced any of them again, he would have to shoot, or numbly accept whatever they wanted to hand out to him.

That would be plenty, he thought grimly. The original shock of Travis's announcement that Lige was no longer a member of the family was gone, and Lige felt more freedom than he could remember. The only sense of loss he knew was for the possessions he left behind him. Everything he owned except for the clothes he wore and the horse he rode was back there with Travis.

Lige had left the main road and chosen a small lane, but he felt safer here. There was little chance he would run into anybody at this hour of the night, and that was all to the good. He didn't want anybody reporting to Travis that they had seen him.

Lige kept heading away from town. He hadn't even briefly considered riding into Lander. He couldn't see where it would do him any good. Oh, he could relate to Duncan everything that happened, and Duncan would be properly sympathetic. But what could he actually do for Lige? Outside of offering Lige a night's sleep in a cell, Duncan was helpless.

Lige looked curiously about him. Damned if it didn't look

as though he had gotten himself lost. The darkness of the night made it more difficult to discern where he was.

"It doesn't matter," he muttered aloud. He wasn't headed in any particular direction. He idly wondered what his ultimate destination would be. Texas, he thought, or he might even drift on down into Mexico. He spoke aloud to cover the pangs he felt at the possibility of leaving a familiar country. "Never did like Wyoming winters anyway," he said.

He paused for a moment as he saw the house, sitting to his right just a little way off of the lane. He had really gotten himself lost. He didn't know that house at all.

For a moment, Lige stared wistfully at the little house. Whoever lived there was asleep, for the house was dark.

He started to move on, then stopped. A spot of light appeared in the house, but it was in the wrong place. That flickering light was on the ridgepole, near the chimney.

"Hell," he exclaimed aloud, "that house is on fire."

Lige turned his horse toward the house and sank his spurs. Even in this short interval the flame had grown. In this isolated area fire was a dreadful thing. Like a sneak in the night, it could wipe out everything a man possessed without his even being aware of it until it was too late.

Lige jumped off before the door and pounded on it, yelling at the top of his voice, "Fire, fire!"

He waited long enough to be sure he heard someone stirring inside. "Fire!" he yelled again. "On the roof."

He couldn't wait here longer until whoever was inside answered his yelling and knocking. In their confusion, they would fumble about, trying to sort out their startled thoughts, while with every second the fire got a firmer grip on the house.

Lige ran alongside of the house. From here he couldn't see the fire, but he could smell it. This was a one-story house, not imposing in size or structure. This was a house built by a man who was struggling to survive.

Lige reached the end of the house. The eaves were just above him, and he jumped up and gripped them. He muscled himself up onto the shingled roof, praying the shingles were not rotten enough to break and drop him back to the ground. He made it and lay there for an instant while he regained his breath.

He hurried up to the ridgepole, and now he heard the crackling of the flames. It wasn't a big fire as yet, but in a few more minutes the flames would engulf the roof.

Lige stripped off his jacket as he reached the perimeter of the fire. He beat at it furiously, flailing away until his arms ached. He beat the flames back to the metal flue extending from the roof. His lungs labored, but he was winning.

Lige paused to catch his breath. God, how fighting fire ripped out everything a man had in him. He wanted to sink down to the roof and rest, but beating out the surface fire wasn't the complete answer. He suspected the fire's origin lay in that metal flue. It had probably rusted out, and a spark from the cookstove below had found an egress in the weakened metal and lodged in a vulnerable spot.

"Hey," a voice called. "Where are you?"

"Up here. On the roof." Lige looked down at the indistinct figures of a woman and man. "It was burning pretty good, but I think I've got it out for now. But I don't know what's smoldering down beside the flue."

The man swore passionately. "I knew that damned flue was rusting out, but I kept putting off replacing it."

Lige impatiently shook his head. Standing here discussing the source of the fire and who or what was to blame wasn't getting them any place.

"Get me some water so that I can douse it down," Lige called.

"Sure thing," the man replied. "Should I come up? I'll get a ladder."

"Not necessary," Lige called cheerfully. "Just get me that water."

The man ran to a well, and Lige heard the creaking of the windlass. He came back carrying a filled bucket with a length of rope attached to it.

Lige went down the sloping roof, planting his feet carefully. A careless or misplaced step, and he could fall off the roof.

The man tossed up the end of the rope, and Lige pulled up the bucket, hearing the sloshing of the water. He swore as the bucket caught on the edge of the roof, and he kneeled to lift the bucket beyond the edge. With all that sloshing and spilling there was only about a half-bucketful left.

"I'll need more," he said. He still didn't know who the man and woman were. Their faces were only pale ovals in the darkness.

Lige took hold of the bail and reclimbed the slope to the flue. He emptied the bucket of water all around the flue and heard the sullen hissing of hot, charred wood.

He came back to the roof's edge and tossed the bucket down. "Get me three or four more," he said. "Some of the water will probably leak down into the house."

"That's better than a fire," the man said. "Mister, I can't tell you—"

Lige cut him short. There would be time enough for thanks after the danger was over.

Lige made three more trips to the ridgepole before he was certain the fire was extinguished. He no longer heard the sullen hissing.

The man below saw Lige moving to the roof's edge, for he called up, "You wait up there until I get a ladder."

Evidently the ladder wasn't far away, for the man was back shortly carrying a homemade ladder. He grunted as he lifted it and leaned it against the roof.

Lige climbed down, and he had hardly touched the ground before the man said, "Mister, I can thank you now. We never heard nor smelled a thing."

He stuck out his hand, and Lige grasped it. It wasn't a big hand, but it felt hard and competent.

"I just happened to be passing by when I saw the fire flickering up there. I knew that was a wrong place for a fire to be."

"How'd you get up there?" the man asked curiously.

"Just hauled myself up," Lige replied. "I was glad those

shingles didn't give away. I stomped and beat out the flames with my jacket. They were just beginning to get a good bite." He looked ruefully at his jacket. It was burnt and blackened in several places.

"Mister—" The man paused, waiting for Lige to give him a name.

"Pa," the woman cried. "He's Lige Matlock."

Lige looked at the woman who had stepped down from the stage, the woman Hamp manhandled.

"Lisa," he said astounded.

The relief from tension made her laugh shaky. "You didn't know me in town, but I recognized you. Pa, I told you about him saving me from being embarrassed."

This was Cleve Denvers, and Lige felt the sudden strain spring up between them. He had only seen Denvers a couple of times, and this was the first time he could recall ever speaking to him.

Denvers knew who he was, and the age-old animosity lay thick between them.

"Well," Lige said, trying to break the awkward moment, "there's not too much damage. You're going to have to replace some shingles, and you have to do something about that flue before you light a fire in the stove again."

"I'll take care of it," Denvers said stiffly. He was on the small side, not any taller than Lige, and his face was lined and worn. From both work and worry, Lige thought.

Neither Lige nor Denvers had anything to say. There was no sense standing here making each other more uncomfortable. "I guess I'll be getting on my way," he said.

"You will not," Lisa said indignantly. "Pa, what's wrong with you? He saved our house. Are you going to let him ride away without asking him in?"

"He wouldn't want to enter a sheepherder's house," Denvers said gruffly.

"You said that. I didn't," Lige replied. He stole a glance at Lisa. How could he ever forget her? He knew the answer to that. This wasn't the same girl he knew the last year he attended school. Comparing that girl with the Lisa he saw now was like saying a caterpillar was exactly the same as a butterfly.

"You can come in, if you want to," Denvers growled and stalked toward the door.

"What am I going to do with him?" Lisa asked in exasperation.

"Don't blame him." Lige sprang quickly enough to Denvers' defense. "After what he's known, I can't say I blame him."

Her face sobered. "Those were bad years, Lige. Do you suppose they're ended?"

"I hope so," Lige said gravely, though he had his doubts. Wounds might heal, but scars were always left, and with. those scars was suspicion. The lasting animosity between two kind of stockmen was what had gotten him into trouble.

"I never properly thanked you, Lige," Lisa said. "I wasn't frightened, just mad. And I didn't know what to do."

"I'm only glad I was there to take care of it for you," Lige replied.

Her eyes twinkled mischievously. "Even more than I expected you to do?" she asked.

Ah, Lige thought, she saw me hit Hamp. He started to explain that wasn't for her but only to save his own hide. He reconsidered. Maybe it wouldn't be smart to tell everything he knew.

Denvers had lighted a lamp by the time Lige and Lisa walked into the house. Lige smelled the disagreeable odor of burned wood and smoke. His dousing of the flue had been thorough. Maybe he had poured in too much water, for it had soaked through the ceiling and trickled down the walls.

"Sorry about that," Lige apologized, indicating the stains. "But I had to be sure it was out."

"Did you hear any complaints from me?" Denvers asked sharply.

Denvers hadn't taken time to dress. He had pulled on a pair of trousers over his nightshirt and wore a pair of untied shoes. Lisa's appearance showed the same haste, for she wore a robe over her gown.

"Sit down," Denvers offered, gesturing almost angrily at a chair. "I can't even offer you a cup of coffee."

Lige wondered if Denvers' anger was directed at the fire or at him. Probably both in equal proportions, he decided. Denvers had too many unpleasant memories rankling him to feel comfortable around a cattleman.

"Don't need it anyway," Lige said. "A smoke will do me just fine." He rolled and lit a cigarette. He didn't know what to say to break the tension between them. Shouldn't have come in here, he accused himself, but Lisa had made her invitation too strong.

"I am grateful," Denvers said. He stared steadily at the table, refusing to look directly at Lige. "My house could be burning up by now, if you hadn't been passing by."

"You don't say that as though you're grateful," Lisa said tartly. "All I told you was that Lige saved me embarrassment after I stepped off the stage. I didn't tell you who the offender was because I know how wild you can become." She drew a deep breath to steady her voice. "It was Hamp Matlock, Lige's brother."

Now Denvers looked at Lige, his eyes narrowed and piercing.

"Dear God," Lisa said, shaking her head. "What does it take to prove to you that every cattleman isn't automatically against you? Lige hit Hamp over the head with his gun barrel. The last I saw of Hamp he was stretched out cold."

Denvers' eyes widened, and the piercing quality was gone. "You did that for Lisa?"

Lige smiled wryly. This was as good a time as any to start being honest with these people. "I stepped in because I don't like seeing any woman molested. But then it turned into a purely personal fight. The sight of my drawn gun didn't bother Hamp at all. He said he was going to take my toy away, then beat the hell out of me." Lige's lips were a tight line as he remembered his indecision as he stood before that jeering crowd. "Hamp's done that all of my life. I couldn't allow it to happen again."

"Ah," Denvers said, and there was a lot of understanding in that simple word.

Lisa shook her head, and sympathy poured from her.

Lige smiled in genuine enjoyment. For the first time he could believe Denvers wasn't so completely set against him.

"Say!" Denvers said suddenly. "Something just occurred to me. Pancho was jumped by three of Harley Inman's riders. They knocked him down and were kicking him to pieces when a fourth man interfered. Pancho was pretty sick. He didn't know who the stranger was. But he's certainly grateful to him. He remembers that stranger shooting one of Inman's men. Say," he said, with a sudden look of illumination, "Pancho describes him as being about your size. Was that you?"

"Aw," Lige said in quick embarrassment. "What else could I do? Stobie drew on me. I had to stop him."

"Stobie Inman?" Denvers asked.

At Lige's reluctant nod, he whistled sharply. "Hell man, he's got a reputation with a gun."

The shine in Lisa's eyes bothered Lige, and now it was his turn to look at the table. "Damn it," he said. "I couldn't stand by and watch three men kick a defenseless man to death."

"A lot of people on your side could," Denvers stated. But the words were soft, carrying no implied criticism. "I'd say you built up a lot of ill will with some people."

Lige grimaced at the memory of that brief, ugly scene with Travis, Hamp, and Ordie.

"I found that out," he confessed, "when I returned home this evening." He looked from Lisa to Denvers. He might as well tell all of it. It wouldn't be long before the entire countryside would be talking about it. "Travis told Hamp and Ordie to beat some sense into my head," Lige said slowly. "I'd made up my mind that kind of handling was over. I've taken too much of it."

Lige looked at them again and went on in a slow, measured tone. "I'm not big enough to stop Hamp and Ordie. I drew on them. Even the sight of my gun didn't stop them. All they could think about was getting their hands on me. Hamp had the same idea in his mind before, but this time was different. I couldn't knock both of them out."

"You shot them?" Lisa asked breathlessly.

Lige wondered if that would have made a big difference to her. "No," he said. "But I had to fire a bullet into the floor close to Hamp's foot." Lige's grin had no warmth in it. "For a few seconds, I guess Hamp thought I'd shot his foot off. But Hamp and Ordie backed off. That drove Travis wild. He threw me out for good."

"Your own father threw you out?" Denvers asked in shocked tones.

Lige shook his head. He hesitated, but he might as well get it all out. "I found out Travis isn't my father. He only raised me."

"How awful," Lisa whispered.

Lige glanced sharply at her. The last thing he wanted from her was pity.

"I'll live," he said shortly. His grin came back a little stronger. "So you see I'm not a Matlock. Travis did tell me who my real father was. I'm Lige Madison."

Denvers stared at Lige with an odd look weighing in his eyes.

Finally Lige said, "Go ahead. Say it."

"I was just wondering if you were headed anywhere in particular," Denvers said mildly.

Lige held out his hands in a futile gesture. "It doesn't matter now. I'll find something to do someplace."

Lisa and her father exchanged a glance, and Lige felt as though he was being judged unfairly. Evidently they reached some conclusion. Lige stood. He wasn't going to sit here and be weighed.

"I'll be going," he said.

Denvers grinned up at him, the first time Lige had seen him smile since he came in here. It softened the homeliness of his face and erased some of the lines of worry.

"Don't be in such a hurry," Denvers said. "Were you looking for any kind of a job in particular?"

Lige stared at him. What was Denvers driving at?

"A riding job," Lige said flatly. "Some spread that needs help." Again, Lige was aware of that silent judging. "I'm a fair hand," he flared. "I can earn my way."

Denvers drew a deep breath as though he had suddenly reached a decision. "I have no doubt of that," he said gravely. He looked at Lisa again, and this time Lige saw her nod. Evidently Denvers and his daughter had reached a mutual agreement.

"Would you consider going to work for me?" Denvers' words ran together as though if he couldn't get them out fast enough, they wouldn't come out at all.

"With sheep?" Lige's tone and expression showed his astonishment. "I don't know the first thing about sheep."

Lisa leaned forward. "You could learn, couldn't you?" she asked softly.

Lige's legs felt weak, and he sat down again before they refused to support him. "What could I do?" he asked helplessly.

"I need somebody to drive supplies around to the sheepherders' wagons," Denver replied. "Don't tell me you can't drive a wagon."

Lige blinked several times. "Hell yes, I can drive a wagon," he said. The offer left him limp. Maybe Denvers wasn't looking at this squarely. Lige could see a lot of problems ahead that evidently Denvers couldn't see. "You could be heaping a mess of trouble on your head," he warned.

"I know," Denvers said patiently. "You've been a cowman. A lot of people will consider you a turncoat. Does it bother you that you might be heaping that trouble on your own head?"

Lige responded to the twinkle in Denvers' eyes. It was good to feel wanted again. "Not too much," he said and grinned. "I don't know any law that says a man can't do whatever he wants."

Denvers rubbed his hands together as he beamed. "You

don't know how hard it's been for me to hire help. You keep putting me in your debt."

"No," Lige said and shook his head. "You've just evened up the score."

"You'll stay here," Denvers said positively.

Lige grinned in pure pleasure. He didn't know that in saving a house he was also giving himself a roof over his head. His face sobered as he thought of what could lie ahead. My God, how Travis would roar when he learned about this. His jaw hardened. Travis couldn't get any angrier than he had before, could he?

"You've just hired a hand," he said. Still, that little hollow in his stomach persisted. He suspected that it would be with him for quite a while. Lisa was smiling approvingly at him. Lige erased the premonition of trouble ahead. Wasn't life always that way? When one problem was solved, a dozen others took its place.

CHAPTER EIGHT

Lige found himself humming as he toted a bundle of hand-hewn shingles up the ladder and onto the roof. Denvers had told him before he left for town that he would find the shingles, a hammer, and nails in the shed behind the house.

Lige laid the shingles down and surveyed the area around the flue. In the darkness, he hadn't been able to determine the full extent of the damage. He shook his head dubiously. He just hoped he had enough shingles to replace the burned ones, but it was going to be close.

Lige was strangely at peace with the world as he ripped off the burned shingles and tossed them off the roof. He had lain awake a long time, thinking of his talk with Cleve Denvers. Last evening before he passed Denvers' house he would have scoffed at the possibility of completely changing his viewpoint. What was happening to him was like denying everything he had ever felt or had been taught. Now, he stood on the opposite side of a wide chasm with Travis, Hamp, and Ordie glowering at him from the other side. He should know a fear, and certainly considerable worry about what was going to happen, but oddly enough, he felt neither. He was wanted here, and he was needed, and if that wasn't enough to bolster a man, he didn't know what was.

Lige was no expert at laying shingles, but he could see how the old ones had been placed. If he couldn't figure how they were laid, then Denvers should kick him out.

He knelt down and began working, keeping up that tuneless humming. The first row of shingles came out exactly right at the roof's edge, and Lige grinned with pleasure. He didn't even have to whack off a portion of the last shingle, though he had brought a hatchet with him.

"Hey," Lisa called. "Come down from there."

Lige straightened until he could see Lisa standing several feet from the house. Damned if she didn't look fresh and pretty this morning.

"Did I wake you up?" he asked in instant contriteness.

Her laughter was a gay peal of sound. "How could anybody sleep with a heavy-footed ox clumping all over the roof?" At Lige's look of distress, she laughed again. "No, I was awake. I heard you go out. What do you think you're doing?"

He owed her something for making him sweat, and he said gravely, "If I saw somebody on a roof with tools in his hand and I heard him pounding away, I'd say he was fixing the roof."

She made a face at him. "Touché."

Lige didn't know what that word meant. "Does that make us even?"

"Even," she assured him. "Come on down here?"

"Yes, ma'am. Right now, ma'am." Lige climbed down the ladder and stood before her. "Is there anything else you want, ma'am?"

She frowned at him. "What do all those 'ma'ams' mean?"

"You're my boss, aren't you?" Lige said, keeping his face straight. "I guess you've earned the right. Anybody with that much education—" He sighed and didn't finish.

"Oh, stop it," Lisa countered. "I didn't want to go East to school. But Cleve insisted that somebody in this family would be something more than just a sheepherder. Does it bother you, Lige?"

"No," he said honestly. "Maybe a little envious," he added. "It makes a man feel plumb ignorant around you."

She thrust out a hand. "Do we stop sniping at each other?"

"A deal," Lige said promptly, squeezing the firm, small hand. He held it as long as he dared. "That doesn't feel like the hand of an educated woman."

She tugged at her hand to free it, while color spread over her face. "I thought we made a deal."

"I wasn't breaking it, Lisa. It's just that—" Lige paused, at a loss for further words to explain what he meant.

"That I don't seem to belong here?" Lisa challenged. "Dear Lord, Lige, if you knew how much I hated every moment I was away. . . . I'm afraid they didn't pound much into my head. I felt as though I was choking back there. Everything's so crowded. I couldn't escape a moment to be free with my own thoughts."

Lige's eyes were quizzical. She said she hadn't learned much, but she sure didn't sound like it. Lige had never talked to another woman who could handle words as well as she did.

"Poor Cleve," Lisa said and sighed. "I'm afraid he's wasted his money."

"You're not going back then?" Lige couldn't say why the answer to that question meant so much to him.

"There's going to be a fight when I tell Cleve I'm not going," Lisa replied. "But I knew when I left, I was never going back. Lige, it was like being in prison."

Lige thought he understood what she was trying to say. There were all kinds of prisons. Living in Travis's house had been one. Lige remembered how good he felt when he awakened this morning. A sense of freedom was a heady thing.

"Maybe he won't argue too much," Lige said.

"It won't do him any good," she retorted.

Lige grinned at her reply. She had a toughness all her own.

"How about some breakfast?" Lisa asked.

Lige's stomach must have had ears, for it rumbled at the word breakfast. It couldn't be much of a breakfast, for until the flue was replaced, she couldn't use the stove.

She guessed at Lige's thoughts. "It'll have to be a cold one," she warned.

"Anything will do just fine," he said heartily.

He walked into the house behind her. The smell of the fire still persisted. Lige sat down at the table, and Lisa placed a sandwich before him.

"Don't be judging me by this," Lisa said. "I like to cook, and I'm a good one."

"I'll bet you are." Her spirit was constantly delighting Lige.

He started to bite into the sandwich, then paused as a thought struck him. It was logical to think that a sheep ranch would have only one source of meat.

He replaced the sandwich on the plate and said carefully, "I'm not as hungry as I thought I was."

Her eyes danced from inner amusement. "You're also a liar. Why don't you say what's bothering you?"

Lige gulped before he asked, "This is mutton, isn't it?"

"It is not," she replied sharply. "It's roasted leg of lamb from last night's supper. Don't tell me you don't like it. I'll bet you've never tried it."

"I haven't," he confessed. His tone said that didn't make any difference.

Her eyes changed color when she was upset or angry. Usually they were a sparkling blue, but now they had a steel-gray cast to them. They looked like an ominous winter sky.

"I thought you were a fair-minded man," she said tartly. "I see that I was wrong. You've been trained a certain way for so long that your mind tastes before your tongue."

That stung Lige, and he said heatedly, "That isn't so. I'll try it, but—"

"But you know you won't like it," she taunted him.

Lige flushed as he took a cautious bite of his sandwich. He chewed it, knowing his throat would close and refuse this food. His eyes widened as he looked at Lisa. "Say, this is good. It's got a different taste than beef. It's like—" He searched for a description of the taste and couldn't find one. "It tastes like lamb," he said and grinned.

Her eyes were changing shades again; the blue was coming back. She smiled and said softly, "I'm glad you can stand it. I didn't want you to go hungry."

Lige rapidly made inroads in his sandwich.

"I don't suppose you could stand another one?" she teased.

"I sure could," he said happily.

He watched her deft hands slice bread and prepare him another sandwich. He knew full well he liked her. He hoped she felt the same way about him.

"You know a lot about sheep, don't you?" Lige asked as Lisa placed the second sandwich before him.

"I should," she replied. "I was raised around them." The impact of his eyes was too intense, and she looked away. "I guess I should feel differently about them than you do." She cast about for something to distract his attention.

"Do you know sheep are the oldest domestic food animal on this continent?"

Lige swallowed before he could answer. "Naw," he disclaimed. "Cattle came first."

She looked at him pityingly. The rosy color was fading from her face. She had the upper hand again. "That's what cattlemen like to think," she retorted. "Cortez brought a handful of sheep with him when he landed in Mexico."

Lige didn't know the name, but that wasn't what astonished him. "Are you saying all the sheep I see around came from a little bunch this Cortez brought with him?"

Her lips twitched with amusement. "Is that so hard to believe, Lige?"

"I'm not doubting what you say," Lige answered. "But I'm telling you this Cortez better keep out of sight of cattlemen. They'd hang him for bringing sheep into this country."

Lisa laughed until tears came into her eyes.

"What's so funny?" Lige asked in an injured tone.

She wiped her eyes. "I'm not laughing at you, Lige. I was just thinking of how far your cattlemen would have to go to get their rope on Cortez. Cortez landed in Mexico several centuries ago."

Lige shook his head. No wonder she laughed so hard. "Lord, you sure know a lot more than I do, Lisa."

"Sure," she said lightly. "I know about Cortez. You tell me what good it does me."

"I don't know," Lige answered. "But I'll tell you one thing. This Cortez sure started a lot of trouble, didn't he?"

"Too much," she agreed. Her eyes were changing shades again. "There's enough room for sheepmen and cattlemen. Why can't they learn to live together in peace?" she wailed. She made an abrupt gesture. "Don't get me wound up on that subject."

"Lisa," Lige said softly, "before I came here, I felt the same way."

She looked at him and quickly averted her eyes. The rosy color crept into her cheeks again.

"Don't you think Cleve has been gone too long?" she asked. "He left so early."

"He hasn't had time to make the trip into town and back." Lige sought for further words to reassure her. "He'll be back any moment now."

"I hope so," she said in a low voice, but the worry still remained with her.

Lige got an insight to the anxiety women knew when their men were gone, particularly if those men were sheepmen. "I told him to stop in at Duncan's office as soon as he got into town." Lige blamed himself for not having gone with Cleve. He hadn't offered for fear he would run into Travis, or the others. "Duncan will keep an eye on Cleve while he's there. He's as worried as you and I are. The last thing he wants is for new trouble to break out."

"I hope you're right," Lisa said. She still wasn't completely convinced.

"I am," Lige said confidently. "I told Cleve to tell Duncan where I am."

To further quell her anxiety, Lige went on, "Duncan will keep an eye on Cleve all the time he's in town. You can depend upon seeing Cleve driving up any moment now." Lige stood up. "I'd better be getting back to work." He could tell by Lisa's expression that he had talked some of the worry out of her.

"Sure you won't have another sandwich?" she asked.

She felt a lot better, Lige could tell by the mirth in her eyes.

"I'm full," he replied. "But I'd eat lamb again."

Her laughter followed him out of the door. It was good to hear a woman laugh like that.

Lige climbed the ladder and went to his work. He didn't feel like humming now. He guessed some of Lisa's worry had rubbed off on him, for he found himself looking up repeatedly to scan the lane to see if Cleve was coming.

Lige had gone just about as far as he could before the new flue was installed. He looked up as he heard the rumble of wheels, and he sighed in relief. Denvers was coming.

Lige was on the ground when the light spring wagon pulled up before the house.

"Any trouble?" Lige asked Denvers.

"Did you expect trouble?" Denvers asked.

"I didn't know what could happen," Lige returned.

A grin softened Denvers' stern face. "Appreciate your concern, Lige. But nothing happened. I went to see Duncan like you asked. That cost me more trouble than anything else." He chuckled at the alarm springing into Lige's face. "He nursemaided me everywhere I went. Every time I looked up, there he was a few feet away."

"I'll thank Cass for that when I see him," Lige said. "Was he alone when you told him where I was?" At Denvers' nod, he said, "Good. The fewer who know where I am the happier it'll make me."

"Duncan fears trouble, doesn't he?" Denvers asked.

Lige was tempted to deny that, then said honestly, "He does. Did you get any back talk in town?"

Denvers snorted. "How could I with Duncan breathing down my neck?"

"What did he say about me working for you?"

"Not much." Denvers' face tightened. "He said for you to watch your step."

That tickled Lige. "Crusty old bastard, isn't he?"

"He is," Denvers replied with fervor. "I'm glad he's not set against me. If he is, he doesn't show it," he amended.

"He isn't," Lige assured him. "Just don't make his job any harder."

Lisa came flying out of the door. "I didn't hear you drive up," she said. "I was busy cleaning."

Denvers winked at Lige. "Gets pretty bad when a man can't go any place without his daughter worrying about him. She frets like an old biddy hen with a single chick."

Lisa cocked her head to one side as she surveyed her father. "You're the sorriest chick I ever saw," she said cuttingly and turned and walked back into the house.

Denvers chuckled. "She covers up her worry pretty well, don't she?"

"You're lucky to have her worry over you," Lige said soberly.

"Don't I know it," Denvers agreed. "Lisa was a great comfort to me when her mother was taken." A faraway, haunted look came into Denvers' eyes, and Lige felt he was reliving a bad time.

Denvers shook himself and said briskly, "Well, that roof ain't going to get fixed with us standing down here."

"It's about done," Lige said. At Denvers' astonishment, he said, "You didn't expect me to just sit around and wait for your return, did you?"

"Ain't that fine?" Denvers said heartily. "I thought you might have carried the shingles onto the roof and have everything laid out, but I sure didn't think you'd go ahead. Should have known what you had in mind when you asked me where my tools were." He squinted appraisingly at Lige. "Looks to me like I hired the right man."

Lige couldn't help but look pleased. It had been a long time since he had received praise of any kind.

"I'm no expert at putting on a roof," he said. "If it doesn't suit you, we can start over."

Lige followed Denvers up the ladder. Denvers kept nodding as he looked at Lige's work. "Hate to say this," he said as he grinned. "But I couldn't have done as well. Looks to me about all we have left is to replace the flue, then fit in a few shingles around it."

Lige felt his spirit expanding. "I saw the flue in the wagon. I'll get it."

"While you're down there, bring up that bucket of tar you'll find in the shed, Lige."

Lige nodded and moved to the ladder.

"Tell Lisa to start thinking of building a fire in the stove. We're going to have a better roof than before the fire. Bet you could stand a hot meal."

"I didn't do so bad," Lige said.

CHAPTER NINE

By the time the roof was finished and the midday meal over, Denvers thought it was too late to start taking supplies around to the herders' wagons.

Lige finished his second cup of coffee. "Never tasted a better meal," he complimented Lisa.

"She's quite a cook," Denvers remarked. "I was afraid she'd forgotten how after being away so long. But she hasn't forgotten a thing." He grinned at Lige. "Never thought I'd see you enjoying a meal of sheep."

Lige chuckled. "Lisa broke the ice this morning. She gave me a lamb sandwich."

"She told you what it was before you ate it?" Denvers asked incredulously.

"She sure did." Lige smiled at the memory. "And I liked it. There was a time when I would've bet that nothing could force me to eat sheep." He shook his head as he asked, "Will man ever get rid of his ingrown prejudices, Cleve?"

Denvers gave the question serious consideration, then shrugged. "He hasn't up to now, has he? We'd have to start raising a smarter bunch of kids, and I haven't seen any indication of it. They start out early hating as fiercely as their fathers." He looked steadily at Lige and murmured, "You're kind of a throwback, Lige."

"I told you Travis isn't my real father," Lige said. "All my life I thought I belonged there. I guess I made Travis so mad he wanted to hurt me with the truth." He grimaced at the memory. "It gives a man a lost, lonely feeling to suddenly realize he doesn't belong. Hell, Cleve," he finished plaintively, "I've got a new last name. It doesn't fit very well yet."

"Does that bother?" Denvers asked.

"Not much," Lige said. "I guess it's a relief to know I'm not a Matlock."

"Kind of a relief to me too," Denvers said wryly. "Let's go check the supplies in the wagon."

Lige was just as happy that Denvers ended that conversation. "Where do you want them put?" he asked.

"Maybe we'd better leave most of them in the wagon," Denvers decided. "We'll take them around to the camps tomorrow."

Lige objected to the prospects of an empty afternoon. It would leave him with too much time to think. "You've got something that needs doing," he said.

Denvers' laugh was a dry burst of sound. "Did you ever see a time around a ranch when that wasn't so?"

Lige kept himself busy with the chores Denvers pointed out. He greased the wagon and repaired and polished the harness. Rebuilding a section of the horse corral took most of the afternoon, and Lige was looking for something else to do when night fell.

"My God," Denvers said. "Don't you ever stop?"

"I like to keep busy," Lige said simply.

Denvers shook his head. "I used to feel that way, but I found a sure cure for it."

"What's that?" Lige asked.

"Growing older," Denvers said sourly.

The sun was just gaining strength when Denvers and Lige started out in the morning. Early arising must have depressed Denvers for he was cross. He had argued with Lisa, telling her there was no need of her fixing their breakfast, but she had insisted. Lige smiled as he thought of the meal. He had eaten ham, flapjacks, and eggs. That girl sure had a way with a fry pan.

"What are you grinning about?" Denvers asked. The crossness was still in his voice.

"I was thinking of that breakfast," Lige replied.

"It wasn't necessary," Denvers stormed. "Lisa thinks this ranch would fall apart, if she wasn't around."

"Maybe she likes working," Lige said quietly.

"Why damn it," Denvers growled, "don't be arguing with me about what is best for my daughter."

"Cleve," Lige protested, "I wouldn't think of—"

"Oh stop it," Denvers interrupted him. He was silent a long moment, then muttered, "She's not fooling me. She's trying to prove I can't do without her. I got along all right when she was gone, didn't I?" Denvers' tone said, go ahead and argue against that.

Lige ignored the challenge. "Maybe she likes what she's doing."

Denvers drew in a rasping breath. "Ah," he said. "She's talked to you about it."

"A little," Lige confessed. "There's all kinds of freedom, Cleve. Maybe this is where she finds hers."

Denvers' face contorted with anger. "I don't give a damn what she feels. She's going back to school. By God, there's going to be one smart one in this family."

Lige wisely kept quiet. This was apparently a sore subject with Denvers. Lige thought of the determined cut of Lisa's chin, the snap in her eyes. Maybe Denvers didn't know it, but he had already lost the battle with her. But there was no use arguing with him further about the matter. Fall was quite a way off. Denvers had ample time to change his mind. Lige almost grinned again. Denvers had a mind against him as tough as his own, maybe even more so.

They rode a long way in silence before Denvers spoke again. "Damned if I can figure out this life. A man struggles to make sure he's going to make it, then he transfers his goal to something else, something better for his family."

Denvers was drifting back onto the subject of Lisa's willfulness again, and Lige thought he'd better change the subject.

"How many head do you have, Cleve?" he asked.

"Eight thousand," Denvers said dourly. At Lige's whistle

he said, "That ain't so many sheep. By a lot of standards, that's only a handful."

"I guess I was comparing it to cattle," Lige said. Eight thousand head of cattle would be an impressive figure. Travis didn't have that many. Lige took his thoughts off of Travis. He didn't want to think of him any more.

"That many sheep ought to make you a good living," Lige observed.

"It would," Denvers grunted, "if I was left alone. First, there's the damned predators. If you knew how many head I lose to wolves and coyotes—" He shook his head and didn't finish the sentence. "A sheep is the most helpless thing in nature. If it's not the wolves and coyotes, it's eagles and lynxes. Everything seems to have a taste for sheep."

"Eagles?" Lige asked in surprise. He had never thought much about them before. Sure, he had seen hundreds of them, soaring and wheeling in the skies, and he guessed they had to eat something, but he hadn't thought lambs were on their list.

Denvers nodded. "A newborn lamb is pretty helpless. I wish I had a dollar for every lamb I've seen carried off by eagles. But I could live with eagles. What they take doesn't amount to a speck of dust in your eye compared to the number I lose to wolves and coyotes. They give me the most hell."

"I can imagine," Lige replied. The same two predators were the bane of cattlemen's lives. Coyotes were sure death for a new calf, but the wolves went after full-grown stock.

Denvers was wound up on his pet peeve. "I chased one wolf for months and never caught sight of him. My God, he cost me enough sheep to stock another ranch." His lips worked wrathfully as he stared ahead. "Sometimes I think those bastards are smarter than man." A thought occurred to him, and he turned his head and squinted at Lige. "You pretty good with a rifle?"

"Fair, I guess," Lige answered. That was an understatement. It was his ability with a rifle that had first caught Brunner's attention.

"I might put you to knocking off a few wolves," Denvers said reflectively. "Naw," he said, shaking his head. "I've got more important things for you to do. The occasional wolf you'd get wouldn't be worth the time.

"After the predators, there's the weather and the weeds," Denvers went on. He grinned twistedly. "I'm full of complaints this morning, ain't I?"

Lige smiled. He had heard Travis complain along similar lines. The same things bothered him, too. Only Travis ranted and raved, using every cuss word at his command.

"You've got to get it off your chest some way, Cleve."

"You wouldn't believe the things that can poison a sheep. Five kinds of death camass can be found all over this country. Just a nibble will kill a sheep. Black laurel is as bad. One leaf will cost you a head."

This was new to Lige, and he listened attentively. If such things bothered cattle, he hadn't heard about it.

"There's more?" he asked.

"That's just a start," Denvers said bitterly. "There's the lupines. Sheep can eat them in early spring, but when the bean pods form, they're deadly. Then there's arrow grass and chokecherry. Worst of all is the locoweed. There's three kinds of that—white, purple, and blue. I guess the white is the worst. If the grass is good sheep will avoid the worst patches. But if they get hungry—" Denvers' shrug finished the sentence. "A good herder keeps an eye out for locoweed, driving the sheep away from it. My God," Denvers exclaimed, "if I had known what I know now, I'd have run like hell the first time anybody even said sheep to me."

He grinned mirthlessly at Lige's expression. "There's more. A lot of plants aren't poisonous but they have sharp spines that puncture the skin, opening a way for fungi. Then you can have lumpy jaw because the sheep can't chew or even see. Things like squirreltail, awn grasses, sticktights, cockleburs, puncture vine, and a lot of cactuses. Other woody plants ball up and cause stomach irritation. You can add pingue, mullein, soapweed to that list. Turkey mullein forms a mass of matter sheep can't digest. I've seen twenty such balls as big as hickory nuts from the stomach of one sick sheep."

Lige shook his head. "I don't see how you raise a single head."

Denvers smiled grimly. "I've wondered about that, too. But I stayed in this business, even though I got a little smarter. Hell," he said wearily, "it wasn't smartness. It was just resignation. I started as a sheepherder. The flockowner gave me the bummies." He laughed at Lige's puzzled look. "Bummies are the motherless sheep, for one reason or another. Maybe his mother died, or she refused to accept him. If somebody doesn't bother to hand-feed that lamb, he dies. I hand-fed a lot of them when I started out."

Lige looked at Denvers with new respect. He could visualize the long, slow struggle Denvers had endured in reaching his present status. Maybe a man could start a cattle herd the same way, but Lige thought it would take far longer than it took Denvers, and that prospective cattleman wouldn't be nearly as big as Denvers in the same length of time.

"You came a long way," Lige said quietly.

"I guess so," Denvers said with no life in his voice. "I got some land and built up my flock. I sent back and imported some Ohio Merino rams. I've doubled the wool production and almost doubled the weight of my marketable lambs. Sometimes, I wonder if it's worth the struggle."

That shocked Lige. "How can you say that?" he cried. "You've got proof that it's paid off."

The bitterness returned to Denvers' eyes. "Have I? Do you think I'd be complaining if I was left alone? Don't you think I know the talk that's running around town? Sheepherders ain't very popular men. I heard that talk everywhere I went, and I saw the looks on people's faces. They looked like they wanted to spit on me."

Denvers cleared his throat and spat over the wagon wheel as though he was trying to clear a bad taste from his mouth. "I guess Duncan being around kept people from opening up on me."

"The storekeepers took your money, didn't they?" Lige asked heatedly.

Denvers' lips twisted in wry amusement. "That was the only thing that made me acceptable."

"Is it ever going to get any better between sheepmen and cattlemen?" Lige asked.

"No," Denvers said abruptly. "You've heard the old saying you can't teach an old dog new tricks. Cattlemen have always hated sheepmen. I guess it'll go on until the last sheep is run off the face of the earth."

"But why?" Lige demanded. "I've listened to you talk. I know cattlemen have similar problems. Both of you are trying to raise livestock to make a living."

Denvers' lips twisted ironically. "Haven't you lived around Travis Matlock long enough to know the answer to that?"

"I want to hear it from you," Lige insisted.

Denvers looked weary. "It's the same old story. Cattlemen say sheep destroy the grass. They say cattle won't eat where sheep have grazed. They claim sheep will destroy their way of making a living."

Lige had heard all those arguments before but solely from a biased viewpoint. Now, he wanted to hear the other side. It could be equally as biased, he told himself.

"Hell no, it isn't true," Denvers shouted. His voice lowered. "Oh, I'll admit that in light, sandy soil sheep might pull up some of the grass by the roots. But they don't eat grass roots as cattlemen claim. They graze close, but that's all. They even improve the grass. The little, sharp hoofs harrow the ground and set the grass seed deeper, and their manure makes the grass better. Haven't you seen that?"

Lige shook his head. He hadn't been around sheep enough to notice anything like that.

"After sheep have grazed, and the grass comes back," Denvers went on, "you've never seen anything like it. The grass is thicker and so rich it looks almost black. I've seen cattle go after a piece of grass like that. But try to convince a cattle owner."

"Are you saying sheep and cattle can be run together?" Lige's tone expressed all the doubt in the world.

"They can," Denvers said. "I've seen it done."

Lige had no desire to call Denvers a liar, but his doubt still remained. "Then why don't you run cattle with your sheep?" Lige asked.

"Why should I?" Denvers asked scornfully. "I can make more money out of sheep. You don't believe that? On the land I have, I couldn't begin to run enough cattle to give me a decent return. So why should I even consider cattle?" His eyes raked Lige. "Damn it, I haven't got enough land for the sheep I want to run. I couldn't get through the year unless I had a lease for summer grazing on the Shoshone Reservation."

Denvers painted a vivid picture, and Lige was beginning to be convinced. All Denvers asked was to be left alone. That wasn't much of a request.

They drove another long way in silence. Denvers pointed ahead and broke the silence. "There's Pancho's wagon."

"Has he already gone back to work?" Lige asked in wonder. "I didn't think he'd be able to work for a week after the beating he took from Stobie and the others."

"He's sore," Denvers admitted. "But he gets around. He'll want to thank you for what you did for him."

Lige shook his head. "It isn't necessary."

"It's better that he knows who you are," Denvers said firmly. "It'll make him know he can trust you. You can't blame him for being suspicious of cattlemen."

"I don't know what I am," Lige said wryly.

Denvers hailed the wagon as he drove up beside it. He didn't get an answer and said, "He's out with the flock. That won't be far. About six miles a day is all a flock covers. Three miles out and three back to the wagon. The sheep are corralled at night. That lets Pancho keep a closer eye on them and cuts down the wolves' or coyotes' raids. The dog has a better chance of smelling them, and he raises hell. Then Pancho can get out and blast away with his rifle."

Denvers grinned ruefully. "Pancho's not much of a shot, but he scares the predators away."

Lige couldn't see a corral anywhere near, and Denvers caught his puzzled look. "We make a corral every night," he said, "out of sticks and long lengths of muslin. I know that sounds flimsy to you, but it'll hold sheep in."

"You couldn't hold a bunch of cattle with that," Lige commented.

"No way," Denvers agreed. "Unless you ringed that corral with a bunch of riders on duty all night. We might as well unload Pancho's supplies into his wagon."

Lige carried the basic staples into Pancho's wagon and set them on the floor. This was the first time he had ever been in a sheepherder's wagon, and he looked curiously about. It was much wider than an ordinary wagon, more like a hut set on wheels. Two people would crowd it, but a lone man could be comfortable enough here. A bunk was at the far end, and a stovepipe extended through the roof from the cookstove on the floor. A table and chair, and a cupboard along one wall completed the furnishings. Lige was surprised at the cleanliness of the wagon and commented on it.

"Be easy for a man living by himself to get careless about his housekeeping," he said.

"I wouldn't keep a man who didn't keep his living quarters clean," Denvers grunted. "A man sloppy about his living habits will be sloppy with his work. I've never found fault with Pancho."

Denvers backed down the wagon steps, and Lige followed him. "I want to look up Pancho before we go on," Denvers said. "I like to hear from my herders at least once a week."

"You see them that often?" Lige asked, as they climbed into the spring wagon.

Denvers nodded. "Your job will be taking supplies around. That's why I wanted to show you where each wagon is."

Lige grinned. He didn't see anything difficult about this job. "I should be able to handle that."

"Never had any doubt about that," Denvers returned.

Lige judged they drove nearly three miles when Denvers said, "They're up ahead of us."

Lige listened before he heard the sound; the bleating of sheep. Denvers had keen ears.

The wagon topped a small rise, and the sheep saw it coming. Lige expected to see them scatter in every direction, but the sheep whirled and dashed into a tight bunch.

"I'll be damned," Lige said.

Denvers grinned. "Did you expect them to stampede at the sight of us? Sheep instinct is to bunch up when they're frightened, unless something prevents it. That's the big advantage of handling sheep. A man doesn't have to cover half of the country finding them."

"It sure is," Lige said with emphasis. He contrasted sheep behavior with what would have happened if these animals had been cattle. It would take hard riding for a dozen men before those cattle were turned.

"There's Pancho in the shade." Denvers pointed out the figure blending so well with the shade of a tree.

Lige nodded. Denvers also had keen eyes.

Lige drove up beside Pancho, and Pancho said, "Buenos días, Señor Cleve." He was a slightly built man. Beside him, Lige would feel tall. Pancho had a quick and gentle smile, and his eyes were soft.

"Everything all right?" Denvers asked.

Pancho shrugged. "Muy bueno, señor. Should it be otherwise?" His eyes crinkled at the corners, as though he expressed some secret inner mirth.

"Only what I expected," Denvers said, and his eyes twinkled.

Lige saw something that was rare, a good, solid bond between these two.

Pancho laughed in genuine enjoyment. "How well I know, señor. If it was not so, you would skin me, a slow strip at a time."

Denvers glanced at Lige. "See how well he knows me."

Lige couldn't help but think of the hours he had spent

around Travis. This was the way a relationship between men should be, each treating the other from a basis of respect and confidence.

"Señor, I did find a few grubs in some of the ewes' heads this morning."

Denvers shook his head. "I was afraid you might. It's about time a few of them showed up. I brought your salt with a few pounds of ashes and sulphur."

"That does not take care of the grubs," Pancho said severely, but his eyes still danced.

"Listen to that," Denvers said in mock indignation. "He still isn't convinced I know my business. I brought you some stove soot. That will take care of your grubs."

"Should I mix the soot with the salt?" Pancho asked with false servility.

Denvers leaned over and whacked Pancho on the shoulder. "You know what to do." He glanced at Lige. "He knows more about sheep than I'll ever learn."

"That is not verdad," Pancho said earnestly. His eyes kept evaluating Lige. Señor Denvers had not yet said anything about this new man.

Denvers remedied that. "Pancho, meet Lige Madison. He'll be bringing your supplies around from now on."

Pancho thrust out a hand. "Señor, I am very happy to know you."

"You should be," Denvers said. "He's the one who kept Inman's riders off you."

Pancho's eyes widened. "Is that so?" he said softly. "I could not see very well at the time." He pumped Lige's hand with greater vigor. "How can I say my thanks?"

"You already have," Lige said and grinned. "It was nothing. I just happened to be there at the right time."

"It is far more than nada," Pancho said, shaking his head. "It is something I can never forget. Some way, I will find the opportunity to repay you."

"Don't worry about it," Lige replied. It wasn't hard to like this man.

"Pancho, anything else you need?" Denvers asked.

"Nothing, señor."

Lige lifted the reins. "I'll be seeing you next week."

"I will look forward to that," Pancho replied.

As they drove away, Denvers said, "I'll never have a better man."

"He's a long way from his native land, isn't he?" Lige asked curiously.

"He is," Denvers answered. "I was down in Arizona, buying a new flock. Pancho helped me drive the flock up. He never went back home."

Lige remembered the shadow darkening Pancho's soft, brown eyes. "Something bad must have happened to drive him away from the land he knew," he said reflectively.

"It did." Denvers hesitated, and for a moment, Lige thought he was going to pour out the story. Then Denvers said, "I'll let him tell you about it, if he wants to. We'd better get moving. We've got three more camps to cover before dark."

Lige thought about Pancho as he rode. In a way, there was a similar bond between him and Pancho. Something had happened to drive both of them away from their familiar surroundings.

CHAPTER TEN

Inman was waiting at his door when Travis, Hamp, and Ordie rode up.

"What the hell kept you so long?" he asked crossly. "I thought you'd changed your mind."

"We've got the whole damned night, haven't we?" Travis snapped. "I ain't changing my mind about a thing."

Inman nodded with satisfaction. "Good. Barnes and Thomas are going with us. Stobie wanted to go, but he can't." His face darkened. "That goddamned Lige of yours—"

He stopped at the ferocity masking Travis's face. Travis looked like a loco wolf.

"I told you he doesn't belong to me."

"Sure, sure, Travis," Inman said, trying to calm him down. He would never mention Lige again around Travis, but he couldn't help but wonder where Lige had gone. It was as though Lige had walked off the world. At least, Inman hadn't heard a word about him.

"Barnes, Thomas," he bawled. "Get those horses ready." He looked up at Travis. "We've got time for a drink," he suggested.

"I don't need no drink," Travis said impatiently. "Let's get on with it."

Inman thought Hamp looked disappointed. Hamp was always disappointed when somebody cut him off from a drink. The big hulk, Inman thought in disgust. Travis didn't have much in either son. Lige might be the only one who was worth a good goddamn, but he was gone.

"Who you going to hit?" Travis asked. "I thought for sure it would be Denvers. That Pancho works for him. He's the one that got Stobie in trouble."

Inman made a hard fist. "God, how I'd like to make Denvers the first one. But Duncan could tie in Stobie's trouble with Pancho and come straight after me. I want to see how it goes before we move on. Litell grazes sheep not five miles from my line. He'd make a good first example."

"I don't give a damn who it is," Travis said. "I just want to be at it. I want to teach all those bastards that this isn't sheep country."

Barnes and Thomas brought up three horses. "Looks like we've got some fun ahead," Barnes observed.

Travis glowered at him. "Maybe it's fun to you. To me, it's a necessity." He waited until Inman mounted, then said, "Lead the way, Harley. You know where we're going better than me."

"Ah," Imman said, "I thought that damned sheepherder would be somewhere around here." His comment was the first word that had broken the silent, grim ride.

Pale, diffused moonlight bathed the scene—the lonely sheepherder wagon and the corral of sheep near it. As Travis listened, he heard the occasional baaing of sheep. He stared at the wagon and the corral, then said, "They make it easy for us, don't they?"

"They do," Inman said curtly. "But we won't get much farther before that damned dog spots us. He'll raise an alarm."

Hamp withdrew his rifle and patted its stock. "Seems to me we got a way to stop that."

"But not before the dog arouses the sheepherder," Inman said. He watched Hamp with narrrowed eyes. He didn't know just how tough these boys of Travis's were.

Hamp patted the rifle butt again. "Same cure for him, too," he growled.

Inman's pleasure showed in his laugh. "You'll do, Hamp." He raised his head and swept it forward.

Six riders moved slowly toward the unsuspecting camp. The dog picked up their scent and started barking before they covered half the distance, and an indistinct figure appeared in the doorway.

"What is it, Shep?" a voice called.

The dog barked furiously.

Hamp snugged the rifle butt to his shoulder, centering the sights on the figure. He squeezed the trigger, and the form was slammed against the door's edge. He clung there for a long moment, and even from this distance, his sobbing groans could be heard.

Hamp fired again, then a third time. The form fell, lying half in, half out of the doorway.

Hamp bared his teeth. "Had to make sure, didn't I? That damned dog is getting on my nerves." He aimed and fired again, and the barking was suddenly snapped off.

"Good work," Inman said approvingly. Maybe he was wrong in underestimating Travis's sons. At least, he was wrong in his evaluation of Hamp.

The shooting had aroused the sheep, and their bleating was a bedlam of sound. They packed tighter and tighter in the middle of the corral.

The six men rode up to the corral and looked into it. "God, I hate the sound and smell of these critters," Hamp said. He emptied his rifle into the packed mass inside the corral.

The riders fired as rapidly as they could pull a trigger. Bullets tore through the helpless mass, and the sheep went wild. Their terrified bleating rose until it was a din hammering at a man's ears. The firing never stopped.

The sheep could no longer withstand the terror. In a concentrated lunge, they broke through the flimsy barrier and bolted in all directions.

"They're getting away," Hamp yelled.

Inman stopped him from spurring after the fleeing sheep. "Let them go. Wolves and coyotes will get most of them." He looked with mean satisfaction at the huddled forms in the wreck of the corral. Here and there a woolly body tried to get on its feet.

"I'm about out of ammunition," Inman said.

Heads bobbed in agreement with his remark.

"I'd say it's a damned good job," Inman said.

"How many do you think we got?" Travis asked.

Inman grinned cruelly. "Litell will have to count them."

"Maybe this will show the bastard he isn't wanted here," Travis growled.

"I hope so, but they learn slow," Inman said. He looked around at the men with him. "Duncan will look into this."

"Won't do him any good," Hamp chortled.

"It will if somebody gets careless with his tongue," Inman said sharply. "All of us have got to have unbreakable alibis."

Travis gave the warning some thought, then nodded. "Ordie, Hamp, and me were busy doctoring a sick stallion. Up all night with the horse."

"Good," Inman said briskly. "I'll figure out what Barnes and Thomas and me were doing. Duncan can beat his head against a stone wall for all the good it will do him."

Travis replaced his rifle in its scabbard before he turned his horse. "I'm glad it's started," he said passionately. "I've waited too long for this night.

CHAPTER ELEVEN

Denvers nailed the board Lige was holding and grunted with satisfaction. "That finishes that job. Been needing to patch the shed for some time, but I never got around to it." His shrug was more eloquent than words. It said, you know how it is.

How well Lige knew. A man never knew an idle moment around a ranch. One chore after another kept pressing for attention. The best anybody could do was to take care of the most demanding ones.

Lige heard the thud of hoofs, turned his head, and stared at the oncoming riders. "Cleve, that's Cass and Harper coming," he said as he recognized them.

"Wonder what they want?" Denvers' voice was suddenly tight.

"We'll find out soon," Lige observed. "They're coming pretty hard." He felt an uneasiness this morning. It took something unusual to pull Duncan and his deputy out here. Lige racked his brain. He couldn't think of a thing that might interest Duncan.

Duncan stepped forward as the two riders stopped. "Howdy, Cass. Jesse," he greeted them. "Looks like something's nipping at your tail this morning."

"It is," Duncan said testily. "Somebody hit one of Litell's sheep camps last night."

"Good God," Denvers cried. "Anybody hurt?"

Duncan was livid with fury. "The murdering bastards shot down Litell's sheepherder. They caught him in the doorway of his wagon and put three holes in him. Then they slaughtered the sheep. Litell reported he found over three hundred of his sheep dead in the corral. The rest of his flock burst out and scattered. Litell didn't take time to round them up before he rode into town. I didn't even have time for a cup of coffee," he said bitterly.

"Jesus," Denvers said weakly. "It's started all over again."

"It looks like it," Duncan said grimly.

"You been out where it happened?" Denvers asked.

Duncan's look told Lige Duncan was filled with a sick rage. Lige appreciated how he felt. He knew a similar rage. He thought of a lonely man stepping to the door after he had been hailed. Not a chance, not a chance. The phrase rang over and over in Lige's mind.

"Jesse and I were there," Duncan said grimly. "By the number of spent shells, maybe as many as a half-dozen men did it. They used a hell of a lot of ammunition."

"Did the shells tell you anything?" Lige asked.

"Rifle shells," Duncan said curtly. "The same caliber everybody around here uses."

Denvers looked as though he was trying to gather his scattered thoughts. "You got any idea who was behind it, Cass?" he pleaded.

"Idea, no more," Duncan replied savagely. "I can't make any arrests with that. I stopped by to warn you to be on your guard. I don't know if this is only an isolated case, or the outbreak of another war. But you know how it can spread. Let people get a taste of blood, and they turn into animals, howling for more. Hell yes, I've got suspicions. I've already talked to the worst sheep haters in the county, Harley Inman and Travis Matlock. But they deny any knowledge of this. I couldn't break them. Both of them have ironclad alibis, unless they're backed up by other good liars."

"You expect more trouble, Cass?" Denvers asked in a small voice.

"I do," Duncan said flatly. "It won't stop until I can catch somebody in the act." His face was despondent. "I've been through this before. It means Jesse and me will wear our asses off. It's a big county, and we can only cover a small amount of it at a time. Oh, goddamn it," he said helplessly.

He shook his head and looked at Denvers. "Cleve, protect yourself all you can. If I were you, I'd put three or four herders at every camp. Arm every one of them well."

"That's fine," Denvers said bitterly. "If I could afford to hire that extra help, where could I find them?"

"I wish I could answer that," Duncan said wearily. "Jesse, let's get back to town."

Lige checked them for a moment. "Cass, Jesse, I'd appreciate you not saying anything about finding me here."

Duncan gave him a long, keen scrutiny. "That's not hard to understand," he said gruffly.

Harper nodded without saying anything.

Lige watched them ride off. He wouldn't want the load Duncan was carrying.

"It's started, Lige," Denvers said, his voice lifeless. "I know it." He started to say more when Lisa came out of the house.

"Wasn't that Cass Duncan and his deputy?" she asked.

For a moment, Lige thought Denvers wasn't going to answer her, then he nodded. "Yes," he said dully.

"What did they want?" Lisa asked.

Lige looked at those level blue eyes. It was going to be hard to lie to her.

"They're looking for a horse thief, Lisa," Lige said easily. "For a while, they thought I was the one they were looking for."

"Oh you," Lisa said, flicking the dish towel she carried at him.

Lige ducked the flicking towel and grinned. He had diverted her for the moment at least. "Naw," he said. "Duncan just stopped by to see how things are going."

Those candid blue eyes rested on him, then she nodded. "You do look like a horse thief," she said, and laughed. "Aren't you two getting hungry? Lunch will be ready in a few minutes."

"We'll be there," Lige said.

He waited until Lisa disappeared into the house before he

looked at Denvers. "Would it have done any good to make her worry?" he asked reasonably.

"I guess not," Denvers muttered. "My God, what are we going to do, Lige?"

"I'm going to take more ammunition out to the herders," Lige said decisively.

"You think that will do any good?" Denvers asked dispiritedly.

"Maybe not," Lige said. "But at least they'll be warned. They'll know what they can expect."

CHAPTER TWELVE

It was almost dark before Lige reached Pancho's wagon. He had stopped at the other three camps first, giving each sheepherder additional ammunition and telling them in dispassionate tones what had happened to Litell's sheep. The two younger herders showed fear in the tightening of their faces and the harried flash in their eyes.

"We're hoping nobody hits you," Lige tried to assure them. "Duncan's doing everything he can to prevent anything like that happening again."

"A man can't see very far at night," one of the herders had muttered.

Not wishing to add to the herder's natural apprehension, Lige said nonchalantly, "If you want to quit, Cleve will understand."

Lyons considered the proposition for a moment, then shrugged. "I guess not. If there's going to be trouble, I'd have to get out of Wyoming to avoid it. I'm pretty broke to do any traveling."

Lige was stony faced as he waited for Lyons to go on. He hoped his own feigned confidence would influence the herder's decision. "Make up your mind," he said indifferently.

Lyons' attempt at a grin was a failure. "I'll stay. But I tell you this. I won't be doing any easy sleeping for a while."

Lige felt relieved. Lyons was only showing normal fear. "Who could blame you?" Lige replied.

The third herder, Tom Collins, was well into his sixties, but still surprisingly spry and active. He listened to Lige relate the news Duncan had brought, his face impassive.

"Lyons wasn't very happy to hear about it," Lige said

ruefully. "For a moment, I thought he was going to quit." He watched Collins closely. He didn't see any undue concern on Collins' face.

"Can't say I blame Lyons," Collins said judiciously. "Hell, if I was as young as him, I'd be sweating, too. He hasn't seen it all. I have. When he gets a little older, he'll realize there isn't anything new. Only the same things over and over but harder to accept."

Lige couldn't help chuckling. "Doesn't the possibility of more violence bother you?"

"Sure, it bothers me," Collins said honestly. "No matter how old a man gets he clings to life. I've been through this before. I've seen sheep and herders killed in New Mexico. It's happened in Wyoming before. It could happen again." That crusty old face creased in a grin. "But I've learned that most of the things a man fears never happen. Maybe luck will ride with me a little longer."

"I hope so," Lige said sincerely.

Lige waved as he mounted and rode off. The more he saw of sheep people, the more he liked them. They were simple, gentle people only trying to make a living.

Pancho already had the sheep corralled for the night by the time Lige arrived. Lige looked bleakly at the sheep settling down for their night's sleep behind the long muslin sheets. He could visualize what had happened at Litell's camp. Men had poured murderous fire into the packed sheep. Had Litell's herder tried to defend his sheep? Lige grimaced. It was entirely possible. That had been that sheepherder's life work.

A dog barked furiously at Lige's approach, and Pancho appeared in the wagon's doorway.

"Devil," he shouted, "stop that." He peered about in the semidarkness, trying to locate the source of the dog's alarm. His face cleared as Lige approached the wagon.

"Señor Madison," he said, his face showing his pleasure.

The dog never stopped barking, and Pancho shouted, "I will not have it. Do you hear me? It is all right."

The dog still wasn't convinced, and Pancho shouted, "Must I take a stick to you?"

Either the dog understood the words, or the tone meant something to him, for his barking ceased. He crept up to Pancho, whining uneasily.

Pancho tousled the fur on the animal's head. "Señor, do not fear to dismount. Only his name and his bark are frightening. Inside, he is soft."

Lige swung down and approached the dog, his hand extended. Devil sniffed at the hand, then licked it.

"I told you so," Pancho said in triumph. "He only sounds fierce. A stranger upsets him, particularly at this hour."

The few licks of the dog's tongue assured Devil there was no harm in Lige. He raced enthusiastically around Lige, every now and then darting at him with mock ferocity.

"He trusts you," Pancho said, "or he would not behave so."

"Good dog," Lige said, smiling. He couldn't determine the breed of the dog, though he thought there was collie in him.

"The best I have ever raised," Pancho said solemnly. "When he was only this big"—he measured a span of six inches with his hands—"I saw that he was something special. He tried to chew on my hand when his legs weren't strong enough to support him." Pancho's joyous laugh rang out. "I remember saying, why you little devil. That name stuck."

His face sobered. "But you did not come this far to talk about my dog."

"I didn't," Lige agreed. He hated to disturb this placid man, and he searched for words to put his warning gently.

"Come in before you tell me why you came," Pancho said. "I was just sitting down to supper. You will join me?"

"Be happy to," Lige responded. He hadn't eaten anything since morning, and his stomach rumbled at the mention of food.

He followed Pancho into the wagon and looked questioningly at Pancho as Devil started to come in.

"It is all right. I feed him in here." Pancho ladled something out of a steaming pot and placed a dish on the floor.

Lige listened to Devil's greedy slurping. "It sounds and smells good," he said.

Pancho shrugged. "It is only lamb stew. Maybe the señor doesn't like it."

"But I do," Lige protested. "What makes you say that?"

"Because you are not a sheepman," Pancho replied. "I saw that the first time you were here. You have not been raised around sheep."

"No, I was raised around cattle. Does that worry you?"

Once again Pancho shrugged. "There is much bad blood between cattlemen and sheepmen. But it does not frighten me." There was truth in Pancho's simple dignity. "Maybe one day it will be different. But now, it is not so."

Devil finished his meal and looked up hopefully at Pancho.

"No more," Pancho said firmly. "Do you want to make a glutton of yourself? Besides, you have work to do."

He explained as Devil trotted out of the door. "He will sleep just outside the corral, warning me if anything seems unusual."

"He looks like he understands everything you say," Lige said.

"He does," Pancho said earnestly. "We have long talks between us."

Lige could understand that. A lonely man had to have something to talk to.

Pancho pushed the table over to the edge of the bunk and placed the single chair beside it. "Sit here, señor," he invited. He filled two tin bowls and cut off two thick slices of bread. "I made this bread myself," Pancho said proudly. "It just came out of the oven."

"I was wondering what that good smell was," Lige said.

A quick smile flashed across Pancho's face. He squirmed in between the table and bunk and sat down. "I do not know what I would do without Devil," he said. "Dios, the many steps he saves me. I swear that dog knows more about sheep than I will ever learn." He shook his head in wonderment. "He knows what a sheep intends to do before the sheep does."

Lige dipped a spoon into the stew and tasted it. "Say!" he exclaimed. "This is good."

Pancho beamed with pleasure.

"You could get a job cooking anywhere," Lige said sincerely.

Pancho considered that, then shook his head. "No, señor. This is where I belong."

Lige shook his head not in disagreement but at the waste of ability. "But don't you ever get lonely?"

"Never," Pancho said. "Aren't there times when you want to be alone with your thoughts?"

Lige nodded. "Yes, but all the time?"

"Sí, señor. It is my way."

Lige didn't try to press this simple man further. He finished his stew and said, "I can't remember when I've ever eaten a better meal."

Pancho acknowledged the praise with a nod. "But you did not come out here to praise my cooking."

Lige drew a deep breath. There was no easy way to break this kind of news. He pulled a box of shells from his pocket and laid it on the table.

"But I have enough ammunition," Pancho objected.

"Maybe not enough for what could be coming up," Lige said. Briefly, he related what had happened to Litell's sheep. He didn't see any drastic reaction to his words. Perhaps Pancho's eyes darkened, but that was all.

"Such a bad waste," Pancho said softly. "So you brought out more ammunition so that I can protect myself." There was sadness in his shaking head. "There is little protection against the evil some men have in their minds." He looked past Lige, and Lige knew Pancho saw something Lige couldn't see.

"I haved lived such a time before," Pancho said, and there was anguish in his voice.

Lige waited for him to go on, knowing that Pancho was reliving a tragic time.

"I had my own flock in Arizona," Pancho went on. He talked as though Lige wasn't in the wagon. "A small flock, but I was building it up. I had a good wife, María."

Lige noticed that both of Pancho's hands were clenched so tightly that the knuckles stood out in stark relief.

"Such a little time I knew her," Pancho muttered. "Less than a year."

His eyes were wide and staring, but he did not see Lige. He looked at an old picture, one that cruelly wracked him.

Lige did not prod him. Pancho was baring his soul, and he was entitled to the pace he chose.

"I had gone into town for supplies," Pancho finally said. "When I returned—" He chocked, blocking his words. When he resumed speaking, his voice was stronger. "María was dead. She lay near the sheep corral, a rifle beside her. She had tried to stop whoever killed our sheep. They shot her, too."

"Oh, Christ," Lige whispered. "Did you ever find the ones who did it?"

Pancho spread his hands expressively. "Who would I look for, señor? There were many men in Arizona who hated sheep. Should I have gone around accusing all of them? What good would that have done?"

Pancho shook his head in answer to his own question. "It was a bad time, one that I did not think I could live through. But I found that a man can learn to live with grief. Its sharp edge dulls. A little later, Señor Denvers was looking for somebody to help him drive sheep north. I was glad for the opportunity to leave the country where I knew only grief."

Now, Lige could understand why Pancho was content to live a lonely life. This was the only bearable life he could find.

"I'm so sorry, Pancho."

Pancho shrugged. "As I said, the years have dulled the pain. I welcome the chance to speak of her. Yes, I think of her often. I try to remember only the good things."

He reached into his pocket and pulled out a wadded-up

handkerchief. He unfolded it and lifted out a massive silver bracelet, liberally studded with turquoise stones. "I gave this to María, the first thing of value I could afford to give her. A Zuñi Indian made it for me, and I told him to spare no cost. María was wearing it when I found her. I thought of burying it with her, but this is the only contact with her I had left. I do not think María minds that I kept this." His eyes begged Lige to agree with him.

Lige's throat was right. "I'm sure she doesn't," he said thickly. He ran the bracelet around in his fingers before he handed it back. "She must have been very proud of it."

"Sí," Pancho whispered. He looked at the bracelet before he wrapped the handkerchief around it and thrust the wadded-up mass back into his pocket. "Never have I been without it. Though I do not need it to remember her."

Lige nodded. "I'm sure you don't."

"So you can see that it does not bother me when you warn me more trouble might come."

Lige was worried. Was he imagining a fatalistic tinge in Pancho's voice? "But you've got to protect yourself."

"I will protect the sheep," Pancho said. His smile was true. "That is my job. Perhaps nothing will happen."

"I hope so," Lige said as he stood. "Sheriff Duncan is doing everything he can to see that something like this doesn't happen again. But—" His hesitation expressed the doubt he felt.

"But the law is spread so very thin," Pancho finished for him. "And the darkness covers so many things."

Lige was now positive that was a fatalistic tinge in Pancho's voice.

"I'll be out here as often as I can," Lige said.

"You will always be welcome, señor."

Lige's face was somber as he rode toward Denvers' house. How in the hell did anybody stop a few men whose thoughts were twisted and warped? He cursed until all the protest drained from him.

CHAPTER THIRTEEN

Denvers was waiting when Lige returned after his second trip to Pancho's wagon in the last four days. Denvers' displeasure showed in his face.

"Where in the hell have you been?" Denvers demanded.

Lige couldn't blame him for being short-tempered these days. Part of Denvers' irascibility could be placed on the fact Lige hadn't told him where he was going either time.

Lige swung down. "Been out to see Pancho," he said quietly.

"Is that where you were the other day?" Denvers asked. At Lige's nod he said roughly, "Will you tell me why it's necessary to ride out there every couple of days?"

Lige hesitated about telling Denvers his reason for seeing Pancho so often, but Pancho hadn't asked him not to say anything. Lige guessed it would be better if Denvers knew all about it.

"Cleve, Pancho told me something that got to me." Briefly, Lige related Pancho's story. "Even after all that, he still isn't worried about trouble touching him again," Lige finished.

Denvers' eyes darkened as Lige spoke. "He never told me a damned word about his wife," he muttered.

Did Denvers resent being shut out of Pancho's confidence?

"Maybe he saw no reason to bring it up before," Lige said evenly. "He wasn't trying to get sympathy from me. He was only saying that whatever happened couldn't frighten him."

"The poor bastard," Denvers growled. "So you've been riding out there, trying to protect him."

Lige bristled at the criticism in Denvers' voice, and

Denvers cut him off. "Don't you think I know how you feel?
But you can't do any real good. Even if you stayed out there
twenty-four hours a day, you wouldn't really accomplish
anything. If they want to hit Pancho's camp, the two of you
couldn't stop them. Whoever is trying to stir up trouble is
not coming alone. You heard what Duncan said. He thought
at least a half-dozen men hit Litell."

"Are you saying nothing can be done?" Lige asked incredulously.

"Something like that," Denvers admitted wearily. "If we
could give Pancho the protection he needs, what about the
other three camps? Do we try to protect one camp and ignore the others?"

"Oh goddamn it," Lige cried in frustration.

"I know," Denvers said. "So you see it now. The only way
I know to avoid whatever is ahead, is to turn all the sheep
loose and go out of business."

The helplessness of the situation shook Lige. "I'm still
going to ride out there whenever I can," he said obstinately.

"I want you to." Denvers tried to grin and failed. "I guess
this is what you call getting your ass in a wringer. Come on
up to the house. Lisa should have supper about ready."

Lige felt defeated as he walked toward the house with
Denvers. Now he was beginning to appreciate how Denvers
felt. They were fighting ghosts in the darkness. He sensed
danger all around him, and he was helpless to do a damned
thing.

They came around the house, and Denvers peered down
the road. "Rider coming." His tone was tense.

Lige had already seen the moving figure. "It's Duncan."
His voice was edged by strain. Duncan was riding too hard
for this to be a casual visit.

Denvers waited until Duncan pulled up beside them.
"Don't tell me you're coming out to announce more trouble."

Duncan swung down. His shoulders dropped, and his face
was lined with weariness.

"You're damned right there's more trouble," he said
harshly.

This was a man who was driving himself too hard, too long, Lige thought. "What's happened, Cass?" he asked quietly.

Duncan momentarily ignored Lige's question. "I've been in that saddle so much my ass is numb," he said bitterly. "Four straight nights of riding and not a damned thing accomplished. And he asks if there's been more trouble." He swore steadily, not in wild anger but from frustration.

Lige waited for Duncan to run down. He guessed Duncan had to find some relief.

Duncan caught his breath, then said dully, "Hell yes, there's been more trouble. Hammond came in two days ago and reported saltpeter and blue vitriol had been scattered over one of his flock's grazing grounds."

Denvers' face was ashen, and his eyes were sick.

"What does that do?" Lige asked. He could tell from their expressions it was bad, but he didn't know how saltpeter and blue vitriol worked.

"Both of them are sure death to grazing sheep," Denvers said in a shaking voice. He shuddered as though he could visualize it happening to his own sheep. "Did Hammond lose many sheep? Was his herder hurt?"

"His herder wasn't bothered," Duncan said bleakly. "Whoever was responsible must have slipped in during the night, staying far away from the wagon. Even the herder's dog didn't pick up their scent. Hammond said half of his flock was wiped out. He's got some sheep down sick. He isn't sure they will make it."

"They won't," Denvers said grimly. "Hammond can count on that. If any of his sheep ate that stuff, they're as good as dead."

He looked helplessly at Duncan. "It's getting worse, Cass."

Duncan took that as criticism, for his face stiffened. "Don't you think I know that? Why do you think I'm wearing out my ass? Jesse was so stiff this morning he could hardly walk."

"It isn't doing much good," Denvers said dully.

Duncan wilted under the accusation. Nobody knew that better than he. "No," he agreed. He cleared his throat and spat on the ground. "Whoever is behind this is bound to make a misstep. One little slip-up is all I'm praying for."

Cass Duncan was an honest man, proud of his office. Lige knew how bitter all this must be to him.

"If I could only get my hands on the bastards behind this," Duncan muttered. He glared at Denvers, then at Lige. "Don't you think I know what I see in people's eyes. They're only waiting to see who comes out ahead. They want to be on the winning side. If this keeps up, more and more will join those night riders. Damn it," he cried in a sudden anguish of spirit, "the whole county is ready to blow up in my face."

Lige would never see a man suffer more mentally. Duncan was accusing himself of all his failures, and Lige wanted to say, Cass, you're being too hard on yourself. He wisely kept still. Right now, Duncan wouldn't appreciate anything of the sort.

That self-blame was in Duncan's eyes as he said, "Cleve, I didn't tell you all of it. Dawson had a flock of sheep rimrocked last night. Whoever did it got the whole bunch." His face twisted with self-recrimination. "As usual I was in the wrong place."

The term rimrock was new to Lige, and he looked questioningly at Denvers.

"Somebody drove Dawson's sheep over a cliff," Denvers said, his voice so low Lige barely heard him. "A lot of that was done in Arizona when the cattlemen and sheepmen had trouble there."

Denvers looked at Duncan, and his eyes begged for an answer. "Christ, Cass. What am I going to do?"

"I wish to God I knew, Cleve," Duncan said soberly. "All I can tell you is to keep your eyes open. It looks like I can't spread myself thin enough to cover every place. All I can do is to tell you what's happened."

Again, Lige didn't speak, but he knew how galling those words of defeat were to Duncan.

Duncan walked back to his horse and mounted. He stared at Denvers and Lige a long, brooding moment, then galloped off.

Lige wanted to break Denvers' black, frozen silence. "Not very encouraging is it?" he asked wryly.

"I wish Lisa was still back at school," Denvers muttered.

"You better tell her what's happening," Lige said. He check Denvers' outbreak. "She'll know something is wrong just by looking at your face. Is it fair to let her worry without knowing why?"

Denvers' shoulders slumped. "Maybe you're right," he said hopelessly. "If this ain't a hell of a thing for her to return to."

Denvers started for the house, and Lige followed him. He didn't envy Denvers his job of telling Lisa what was going on.

Lisa was stirring something in a pot on the stove when Lige and Denvers entered. She looked over her shoulder and asked, "Wasn't that Duncan talking to you two?"

Lige glanced at Denvers. Lisa was too perceptive. She knew what was going on, or was too damned close to the truth.

Denvers looked as though his words were clogging in his throat, and Lige stepped in until Denvers could clear his mind. "Why yes, it was Duncan," he said. "He just stopped by for a few minutes."

Lisa turned from the stove, her hands clenched, and Lige thought he heard a catch in her breathing. She ignored Lige's explanation, and her attention was focused on Denvers.

She can read Denvers like a book, Lige thought dismally.

"All right, Pa," Lisa said. "What's happening?" Denvers couldn't look at her, and she said fiercely, "Don't lie to me. I know you."

Denvers looked at Lige, mutely begging for assistance.

"It's best to tell her," Lige said. "She knows Duncan wouldn't be coming out here to pass a few words."

"Maybe you're right," Denvers said and sighed. "Honey,

some trouble's broken out. Duncan came out here to tell me that some of the sheepmen are being bothered."

Lisa paled, but her voice was steady. "How bad is it?"

Denvers stared at the floor. "Bad enough." Briefly, he related what had happened to other sheepmen, not going into detail. "Maybe I'm only borrowing trouble. We haven't been hit yet." He looked drawn and so infinitely weary. "But wondering what happens next is driving me out of my mind."

Lige watched Lisa anxiously and saw no sign of panic. She had a tremendous amount of inner control. "Duncan is trying to do something about it?" she asked quietly.

"He is," Lige assured her. "He doesn't want trouble any more than we do."

Lisa nodded almost absently, then began placing the meal on the table. "He'll take care of it," she said.

That didn't bring the response she wanted from her father. "Are you going to do any good worrying yourself sick?" she demanded. "Will you sit down and eat? Do you think going hungry is going to solve anything?"

"You don't realize what could happen," Denvers said dispiritedly.

"I've listened to you talk about old troubles enough," she said calmly. "Now, will you sit down and eat?"

Denvers broke before her determination and sat down. Lige joined him at the table. The meal was tasteless, not because of Lisa's cooking but because of the thoughts that were in all their minds.

Lige got up before his meal was finished. "Not very hungry," he said. He tried to smile reassuringly at Lisa and failed.

He walked outside and rolled a cigarette. He couldn't get Denvers' distressed face out of his mind.

Lisa joined him a few minutes later. "Neither of you ate enough to make cooking worthwhile." Her shaking head said she didn't blame them. "Poor Pa. He's worked so hard to give me all the things he thinks I should have."

"You're the reason he's worried," Lige pointed out.

"I know that. What do you think makes me feel so

guilty?" Lisa's voice dropped to a whisper. "Lige, how bad do you expect it to get?"

"I don't know," Lige replied honestly. "Duncan can see no further ahead than either of us. That's what is driving him so wild."

Lisa slipped her hand into Lige's hand. "Lige, I'm scared."

Lige returned the pressure of her hand. Maybe it was just the strain of the moment that made her seek assurance, but Lige hoped it was something more. His heart was thudding. He wanted to tell her what he felt but was afraid to.

"I'm scared, too," he admitted.

CHAPTER FOURTEEN

Travis blinked in surprise as he, Hamp, and Ordie walked into Inman's house. Three other men were in Inman's kitchen.

Inman grinned sardonically as he caught Travis's surprised look. "You know the boys, Travis," he said.

Travis nodded. Sure, he knew Metcalf, Townsend, and Eubanks. They were all cattle owners, but what were they doing here?

"They're interested in what we're doing," Inman said easily. "They want to see this country cleared of sheep."

Townsend raised an objecting hand. "Wait a minute, Harley. We haven't said anything of the kind yet."

"But you're here," Inman said triumphantly.

Inman poured coffee all around, then laced the cups generously with whiskey.

Townsend tasted his drink and grimaced. "You didn't put in much coffee, did you? We're here to listen. No more."

Metcalf and Eubanks nodded solemn confirmation. They drank slowly, staring owl-eyed at Inman.

"What do you want?" Inman asked sarcastically. "An absolute guarantee that you come out of this smelling like a rose? I think Travis and me have already proven what can be done."

Townsend shifted his heavy bulk uneasily in his chair. "You've killed a few sheep and a sheepherder. That's all. We don't know what Duncan is going to do. But you can bet he's looking for whoever did it. Sheer chance will let him run across some trace of you sooner or later."

Inman hooted with derision. "You hear that, Travis? Townsend thinks Duncan is going to get ahold of us."

"Duncan's already showed he can be pretty tough," Townsend said stubbornly. He winced at a painful memory. "Duncan stamped out trouble seven years ago before it really got a chance to get started. I was arrested and fined heavily for my part in that. I sure don't want to go through that again."

Inman looked at Townsend with disgust. "You got caught because only a few cattlemen joined in. Too many of the others stood around on the edges, waiting to see if you'd win before they joined. That wouldn't have happened if everybody pitched in. That's why we want every cattleman in this time. What can Duncan do? Hell, he won't buck us. He wants re-election next year, and he knows where most of his votes come from."

Townsend was still doubtful, for he shook his head. "I don't know," he said weakly. "I never heard of anything stopping Duncan if he thinks he's right." He reddened at the criticism he read in Inman's face. "Damn it," he said hotly, "I want the sheepmen run out as much as you do. But frankly, I don't think you can do it. Not with Duncan set against you."

"Horseshit," Inman exploded. "He hasn't caught up with me yet, has he? He won't do any better in the future. If a few more of you join in, nobody will be able to stop the tide. It'll sweep every damned sheepherder out of this county."

Inman saw the weakening in the three faces and bored in. At least, all three men listened attentively. "My God," Inman went on impatiently, "Duncan's been riding his ass off, and hasn't he come up empty-handed? All he's got is that hammerheaded deputy. What good can just the two of them do?"

"He can organize a posse," Townsend warned.

Inman hooted at the suggestion. "Who'll ride with him? Sheepmen? They haven't got the guts." He slashed the air with the edge of a palm. "Who's worried about sheepmen?"

Townsend was still unconvinced. "Duncan's liable to stumble across you accidently. Then where will you be?"

Inman poured himself a drink and downed it in a single

gulp. The liquor made his eyes shine. "No way," he said contemptuously. "I keep a man in town to watch Duncan. As soon as Duncan rides off, my man gets back here and tells me which direction he's going. How's Duncan going to catch us?"

"That's pretty smart," Townsend admitted grudgingly. "But how long do you think it will last?"

In disgust Inman spat on his own floor. "As long as I want it to last. When they see how well Travis and me are doing, more cattlemen will join us. Hell, we'll swamp Duncan under. We'll run him right out of office." His impatience came back, and his face twisted. "Are you with us or not?"

"You ain't stampeding us into joining you, Harley. Not yet. We'll stand back for a while and see how it goes," Townsend said. "If Duncan doesn't catch up with you, then we'll talk to you again."

Townsend looked at Metcalf and Eubanks, and they replied with slow nods.

Inman's face burned at Townsend's turndown. "My God," he said passionately, "I never figured you three to be lily-livered."

Townsend's eyes turned hot, and Metcalf's and Eubanks' faces were red, but they didn't comment on Inman's searing evaluation. They let Townsend do the talking for them.

Townsend managed to keep his voice under control. "We're forgetting you said that, Harley. All three of us have been burned by something like you're proposing. It makes a man a little more careful."

The three of them got to their feet and walked toward the door. Townsend paused there and said, "We ain't against you, Harley. I'd like nothing better than to see you drive all of those damn sheepherders out."

"Get out of here," Inman screamed.

Inman sank into his chair after the door was closed. "The sniveling bastards," he raved. "I was sure I could depend on them."

"Does it make any difference?" Hamp asked boldly. "Hell, haven't we proved we don't need them?"

"But it would have made things easier and so much faster," Inman muttered.

"You thinking of dropping our plans?" Hamp jeered.

Inman gave Hamp a savage look. "If I thought you meant that, I'd knock your damned head off." He blew out a hard breath. "It will just take a little longer. With those three with us, we could have hit several sheep camps at once. Now—" He pounded his fist against his thigh in frustration.

"I know a way of making things go quicker," Hamp said. "There ain't no sense wasting all that ammunition and doing all the riding we've been doing. Dynamite will do it a lot faster."

It took a moment for Inman to digest Hamp's words. "Maybe you got a head on you after all, Hamp," he said with new respect. "You got somebody in mind?"

"How about Denvers' sheep?" Hamp asked. "Didn't Barnes tell you that Duncan is riding north tonight? That takes him out of our way." He thought Inman's lack of response was indecision, and he bolstered his argument. "Denvers is closest. Hell, we'd be home and in bed before night."

Inman grinned at Travis. "Damned if you didn't raise a bright boy, Travis."

CHAPTER FIFTEEN

Four riders approached the sheep camp. Hamp had said that one lone man could do this part of the job, but the other three insisted upon coming along.

Hamp held up his hand, stopping the others. He felt giddy with his position of prominence. This was the first time Travis ever listened to him.

"Goddamn it, it's beginning to rain," Ordie said sullenly.

Hamp grinned at him. Ordie was burning real good. "Just a shower," he said. "We won't be out in it long enough to even get wet." He held up a hand. "No closer, or that damned dog will hear us."

"We took care of a dog before," Inman growled. "What's so special about this one?"

"If I can quiet the dog without shooting him, wouldn't it be better?" Hamp asked. "With all this trouble around, the sheepherder is liable to come out of his wagon shooting when he hears his dog barking." He grinned tolerantly at Inman. "Me, I'd just as soon not get any holes in my hide."

Inman chuckled. "That goes for all of us, Hamp. How are you going to take care of the dog?"

Hamp opened a gunny bag and held it close to Inman's nose.

Inman recoiled from the smell. "What the hell is that stink?"

"Rotten meat," Hamp answered and grinned. "Dogs love it, not only to eat but they like to roll in it."

"Good God," Inman said in disgust. "Now he's talking about feeding that damned dog."

Hamp nodded complacently. "Yes. I'm going to feed him

poisoned meat." He grinned broadly. "You know of anything more silencing?"

Inman whistled. "Travis, he's thought of everything. Maybe we'd better let him do all the planning from now on."

Hamp laughed at Ordie's sullen face. This wasn't setting at all well with his brother.

"I'll be back soon," Hamp said. He dismounted and handed the reins to Ordie. "Think you can hold him, Ordie, until I return?" he asked.

Ordie's curses followed Hamp as he walked away carrying the sack. Hamp sure had Ordie's goat staked out.

Hamp approached the corral from downwind. He didn't know how good this dog's sense of smell was, but he could bet its hearing was excellent. All these damned sheep dogs were like that. The wind's direction protected Hamp's approach.

He got as near as he dared to the corral before the dog made a sound. It was only a tentative bark, as though the dog sensed something and was making inquiries about the sound. Hamp stiffened but heard no more barks. Evidently the dog wasn't sure.

He scattered the poisoned meat in a wide arc. A new worry was gnawing on him. He'd look like a damned fool if the dog didn't find the meat.

Pancho's head raised as he heard Devil's bark. He reached for the loaded rifle. Ever since Lige's last visit, he had been on edge. No matter how much grand talk he made, it didn't dispel his uneasiness.

He waited tensely for additional barking but none came.

"Devil speaks only to hear his own bark," Pancho admonished himself. He wasn't surprised to find sweat on his forehead. How easily a man sweat in a time like this.

Pancho stared at the closed door a long moment before he could relax. Ordinarily, he would have investigated a single bark, but these weren't normal times. Pancho knew better than to be silhouetted in a lighted doorway.

He grimaced as he thought of his brave talk to Lige that fear was no longer in him. Dios, what a liar he was. He wondered if a man ever completely got rid of fear.

He spent the next half hour listening uneasily. Imagination was an ally of fear, for he was magnifying even the most normal sounds into something ominous and deadly.

Pancho stiffened as he heard the whining coming from just outside the door. The whining was broken off, and Pancho heard the racking cough and the struggle to breathe.

"Dios," Pancho said, his eyes going wide. That was Devil, and something bad was happening to him. Pancho snatched up the rifle and threw open the door, forgetting all about his former premonitions.

The dog lay at the bottom of the steps. He looked pleadingly at Pancho and tried to get to his feet, but the effort was too great. He doubled up in sudden agony, then stiffened convulsively.

Pancho hurried down the steps. Devil was still breathing, a harsh, rasping sound, growing feebler with each breath, and his eyes were glazing.

"No," Pancho cried in anguished protest. He forgot all about his own safety and leaned his rifle against the steps.

"Devil," he cried. "What is it?" Pancho started to bend over the dog and never completed the motion. A rifle shot rang out, the bullet slamming Pancho up against the wagon. He hung there, his eyes dazed. He never heard nor felt the impact of the second bullet.

Hamp grinned as he lowered the rifle. "Got him," he said triumphantly. "Didn't it work out like I said it would?"

"It sure did, Hamp," Inman agreed. He wished Stobie had been here to see the herder cut down. It would have done Stobie a great deal of good, for this herder had been the start of all Stobie's trouble.

"Let's get at it," Hamp said and pushed himself up from the ground. After the dog went into convulsions, all four of them had crawled to where they could plainly see the wagon.

Inman scowled at the mud on his clothing. "I hope Duncan gets his ass wet in this rain," he growled.

Travis shook his head. "Ain't gonna last that long, Harley." He pointed to a rift in the clouds. The moon was just beginning to shine through. "Just a little shower," Travis finished.

Inman headed briskly for the corral. Travis and Ordie went with him. None of them noticed Hamp angling off, heading for the wagon.

Inman looked with savage pleasure at the sheep packing ever tighter in the flimsy corral. They were alarmed, and their bleating was filled with terror. But so far nothing had caused them to break through the corral.

If Hamp's idea worked, sheep would be scattered all over the county. Inman meant that literally, and he grinned cruelly.

He looked around for Hamp and saw him bending over the crumpled figure of the herder.

"What the hell are you doing now?" Inman yelled impatiently. "Let's get this over."

"Just making sure he's dead," Hamp called back. He quickly searched Pancho's pockets. He never heard of a sheepherder ever carrying much money, but he had to be sure.

Hamp pulled out the wadded-up handkerchief, opened it just enough to see the dull shine of the silver in the light coming from the wagon. Hamp sucked in his breath. He didn't know what the gems in the silver were, but this thing had to be valuable! He stuffed the handkerchief into his pocket before he straightened. He would look at it more closely later. One thing he knew for sure; he wasn't going to share this find with anyone.

Hamp pulled a stick of dynamite from his hip pocket as he walked toward the others.

"He was dead," he said solemnly.

"Hell," Inman said in disgust, "I could see that without pawing over him."

Hamp kept his face stolid. "Just had to be sure," he said. Inwardly, he was laughing at Inman. Inman thought he was so damned smart. He didn't know what Hamp had in his pocket.

Hamp fixed a blasting cap onto the stick of dynamite, then attached a fuse. He had handled dynamite before, but he admitted he wasn't an expert, but that length of fuse should be enough.

"Better get back," he advised.

He grinned as the three men ran like the devil was nipping at their asses. He struck a match, shielded its flame with his hand until it strengthened, then touched the match to the fuse. The fuse spit sparks, and Hamp tossed the stick of dynamite into the middle of the packed sheep. He whirled and ran like hell. He threw himself down beside Inman and waited, his muscles hurting from the tension.

Damn it, he thought, as he waited. Had he made the fuse too long, or had it gone out? He swore at that thought. Maybe it was only seconds, but it seemed like an eternity.

"I thought you knew what you were doing," Inman growled.

"Goddamn it," Hamp flared. He was sick and tired of taking Inman's lip. He didn't know what had happened. Maybe the moisture from the shower had extinguished the fuse. He started to say something when the unexpected blast froze his mouth open. There was a blinding flash of light, and a deafening roar filled his ears. He thought he saw parts of sheep bodies flying through the air, and a heavy, acrid smell filled his nostrils.

He looked at Inman and said scornfully, "You were about to say something, Harley."

"Christ," Inman said in awe. He shook his head as though he was trying to get the ringing out of his ears. "You were right, Hamp," Inman said in open admiration. "That *is* the fastest way to get rid of them."

CHAPTER SIXTEEN

Last night's rain hadn't amounted to much, Lige thought as he rode toward Pancho's wagon. It hadn't done much more than dampen the ground.

Lige stood in the stirrups as he came in sight of the wagon. He was approaching the camp from the west, and the morning sun was in his eyes. He shielded his eyes from the glare. Everything looked normal, but a bad feeling ran up and down his spine like icy fingers. Some instinct told him to look up into the sky, and he exclaimed in shocked disbelief, "Ah God. No!"

Two buzzards wheeled and dipped in the sky. Even as Lige watched, another one came into view. Their presence screamed only one thing; there was death below.

Lige cursed them until he was breathless, though he knew the buzzards were not the cause of death. They were only drawn by it. Basically, they were cowardly birds. They would continue to dip and soar until they were positive no harm would come to them if they dropped to the ground.

Lige dropped back into the saddle and raked the horse's flanks with his spurs. He knew now what he would find with a certainty that sickened him.

Pancho lay at the foot of the steps to the wagon. Lige jumped off and ran the few steps to him. He did not have to make a closer examination to know Pancho was dead. Blood from two bullet holes had dried to a blackish stain, and a horde of flies buzzed away angrily at Lige's approach.

Lige stared down at Pancho, his face blank. The rage was all inside, ripping him apart. He wanted to rave and scream in an effort to find relief from the hurt.

"The dirty, rotten bastards," he finally screamed in an excess of passion.

Lige tried to calm down and think rationally. Screaming against this injustice did neither him nor Pancho any good.

"I'll find them, Pancho," he muttered. There was little conviction in those words, for Lige hadn't the slightest idea where to begin, or whom to look for.

Lige's scowl deepened. Some disturbance had drawn Pancho out of the wagon, and he had carried his rifle with him. Lige groaned in despair. He had warned Pancho of just such a move. His eyes went back to the still form. There must have been a strong reason for Pancho to disobey sound advice.

Lige's eyes narrowed as he saw something he hadn't noticed before. Pancho's pants pockets were turned inside out. Lige squatted down beside him, his expression grim, as he remembered what Pancho had shown him. Pancho had unwrapped María's bracelet, and his words rang in Lige's memory. "This is the only contact I have between us."

Lige shook his head. Whoever had cut Pancho down hadn't left him a thing. They had rifled Pancho's pockets to take the only thing that meant anything to him.

Lige straightened. If he were only granted one request, it would be that he could get his hands on Pancho's murderer.

Lige scanned the lonely, brooding scene, praying he would see something that would point him in the right direction. He had noticed the dog's still form as he rushed up to Pancho, and now, he moved closer to it. There was dried saliva around the muzzle, and the teeth were bared in one last hideous snarl. Lige would say this animal was poisoned. Now, he could understand why Pancho had ignored all warnings and rushed out to give what aid he could to his dying dog.

Lige stared all around him. He could visualize the skulking murderers lying in wait. They had planned well, picking the one sure thing that would draw Pancho out of his wagon.

If Lige didn't get a solid hold on himself, he would be

raving again. He drew in several long, deep breaths, and the threatening rage subsided.

"Look, damn you," he admonished himself.

He scanned the ground. Last night's shower had dampened the earth enough to take and hold good prints. Lige cursed himself. In his wild grief, he had rushed up here, obliterating many of the footprints, but several of them were still clear-cut. He could trace the murderer's approach to Pancho's body. The left boot print was distinctive. That boot had a hole in the sole, and its heel was badly run over.

Lige tracked the prints back to the ruins of the corral. From the acrid smell still lingering in the air and the seared, broken animal bodies on the ground, Lige was certain dynamite was used. Two coyotes slunk away at Lige's approach. Last night's deed made easy feasting for the scavengers.

Lige looked briefly at the carnage. A few orphaned lambs searched for their dead mothers and bleated piteously when they found them. A half-dozen ewes kept a hopeless vigil over their lambs' lifeless bodies. Perhaps some of the sheep had bolted in panic, but the killing had been thorough.

Lige jerked his eyes away from the scene of senseless killing. He couldn't do anything about that now, but he might find something that would point to the men responsible for this outrage.

By the prints, four men had stood just outside the corral before the dynamite was tossed in. He picked out a dozen more prints of the worn sole and the run-over heel. "They left their horses and crawled up close," Lige muttered, "until Pancho hurried out to help his dog."

Lige shook his head. The picture was as clear as he could make it, and a sense of futility was stealing through him. He had the picture, but he didn't have the makers.

He strode back to the wagon and entered. He pulled a blanket from the bunk, carried it out, and wrapped it around Pancho. Lige bent and lifted the blanketed form and carried it into the wagon. He went back out and brought in the dog, placing it beside Pancho.

He backed out of the wagon and closed the door, making

sure it was secure. This didn't finish the chore ahead of him, but he wanted Duncan to see this scene before Pancho and Devil were buried.

He mounted and turned toward town, his face a frozen mask. Perhaps Duncan would be better at making something out of the few facts he had accumulated.

Duncan looked up in surprise in Lige entered his office. He looked immeasurably weary, and his face was drawn and haggard.

"What are you doing here?" he cried. "Do you want to run into Travis and cause me more trouble?"

"I don't give a damn about Travis," Lige said flatly. Harper wasn't in the office, and that was a relief to Lige. He didn't want to say anything about Pancho to anybody but Duncan. At the moment, Lige wasn't worried about Travis, or his two sons, but he knew what Duncan meant. Running into them in town could blow things wide open, but Lige ignored that danger now.

"Something happened to change my mind," he said. "Cass, they hit Denvers last night. They killed Pancho and dynamited his sheep."

Duncan's mouth opened in shocked surprise, but before he could question Lige's report, Lige said hotly, "Yes, I'm sure. I just came from there. I want you to see it."

"Oh my God," Duncan groaned. "I was out all last night. I'm so stiff I can hardly move."

His words didn't upset Lige. Duncan wasn't complaining about what he had to do; he was only stating that he was in poor shape to be pressured harder.

Duncan rose and grimaced at his stiff joints. "Are you going to just stand there with your finger up your nose?" he asked crossly.

Lige shook his head and followed Duncan out of the door. No matter how rough the problem, Duncan could always be depended upon to do what had to be done.

Neither of them spoke very much during the ride. Duncan gave up questioning Lige after Lige kept saying, "You'll see."

Duncan's eyebrows rose as Lige stopped the horses fifty yards from Pancho's wagon.

"We could have walked all the way and saved the horses more effort," Duncan said testily.

"Some tracks I want you to see, Cass. I didn't want them blotted out."

Duncan nodded grudging understanding. He was puzzled, and Lige guessed at the reason. Duncan expected to see a body out here.

"I carried Pancho and his dog into the wagon," Lige said. Just the retelling of that grim task brought all the anger back, and Lige had to slow down to make his words coherent.

"Pancho was lying there." Lige pointed at the ground at the foot of the steps. "They poisoned his dog. I think Pancho came out to help Devil when he heard him whining, and they cut Pancho down."

Duncan listened to him in complete absorption.

"Cass, this is what I wanted you to see." Lige pointed out the print of a left boot with a hole in the sole and a run-over heel.

Duncan squatted down beside the track and studied it. "Shower left the ground in good shape to take a track," he mused.

"When I first saw Pancho lying here, I rushed up to him. The only thought in my head was to help him," Lige said. "I blotted out some of these tracks. Whoever made them walked right up to Pancho."

Duncan studied him intently. Lige was driving at something, but for the life of him, Duncan couldn't see what it was.

"My God, Lige," he exploded. "That doesn't name anybody. Why hell, I'd bet if I looked hard enough, I could find fifty men in the county wearing boots in this shape."

"Probably," Lige agreed. "But only one of them would be a thief. Whoever shot Pancho searched his pockets. I found them turned wrong side out." Briefly, he described María's bracelet and what Pancho told him about it.

"It still adds up to nothing," Duncan said wearily. "Damn it, Lige, the thief wouldn't be carrying the bracelet with him."

"Maybe, maybe not," Lige said stubbornly. "But it does give you something to go on, doesn't it?"

"It makes this track a little more significant than the others," Duncan admitted. "But don't get your hopes up, Lige. At best, it's pretty flimsy evidence."

Lige couldn't deny anything Duncan said, but his determination didn't weaken. "You can keep your eyes open, can't you?" he reasoned.

Duncan sighed and said, "Sure. I want to look at that corral."

He stood there a long moment, looking at the ghastly remains of the sheep. "A hell of a thing, isn't it?" he asked gloomily.

Duncan looked around before he moved on. "Looks like four of them were in on this."

"That's how I make it," Lige answered. "I've got to tell Denvers what happened before I can go into town with you."

"No need for you to go into town," Duncan said in instant protest. "What good can you do there? I don't want you running into Travis or the others."

"I'm going in to tell Anderson to come out and get Pancho," Lige said firmly. "The least I can do is to see that Pancho gets a decent burial."

"I could do that," Duncan argued. He looked at Lige's set jaw and sighed. There was no use saying anything more. Lige had his mind made up.

CHAPTER SEVENTEEN

Anderson's frown deepened as he listened to Lige's instructions on how to reach Pancho's wagon.

"I don't know," he said dubiously. "That's a long way."

Lige stared at him in outrage. "If you're worried about payment, I've got the money," he said indignantly. To prove his intent, Lige took money from his pocket and offered it to Anderson.

It was evident that the payment wasn't the problem, for Anderson still frowned.

"What's your real reason?" Lige demanded. He shook with anger as a new thought hit him. "Are you refusing to bury Pancho because he's a sheepherder?"

Anderson's eyes gave way before the ferocity on Lige's face. "You don't understand," he said desperately. "You see—"

Duncan cut him short. "Tell Lige your real reason," he said ominously. "If you're figuring you can't bury a sheepherder because you get most of your business from cattlemen, I'm here to tell you you're making a big mistake."

Anderson gulped and paled. "I don't understand what you mean, Cass," he faltered.

"I'm promising you one thing you can depend on," Duncan thundered. "You may not stay in business long enough to see which side wins. I'll see that you're closed up. Do you understand me?"

Anderson licked his lips and looked at the floor. "You've got it all wrong, Cass. I'll be only too happy to go out and get the body."

"You'd better be," Duncan growled.

Lige slapped the money into Anderson's hand, his disgust showing.

"Leave it lay, Lige," Duncan warned.

Lige nodded and walked to the door. It was a good thing Duncan spoke up when he did, for Lige felt like trying to strip off Anderson's hide.

"Thanks, Cass," Lige said when Duncan joined him. This blind, unreasoning hatred was springing up on all sides. "Good Lord, Cass," he said in a choked voice, "will it ever stop?"

"That's my job," Duncan said calmly. "To see that it does. But you won't help matters by jumping in because you disagree with another man's opinion."

"You're right," Lige said. He started to step outside, then stopped abruptly.

Duncan caught Lige's stiffening and asked, "What is it?"

Lige pulled back inside the office. "Hamp's coming down the street. I'd just as soon not run into him now."

"You're getting smarter," Duncan said drily.

Hamp passed the doorway without seeing Lige or Duncan. He was whistling softly, and he looked as though he was pleased with himself.

Lige watched Hamp go on by the building, and his eyes were bitter. Here was a perfect example of the same lack of reasoning Anderson had just displayed. Hamp would applaud the manner in which Pancho died.

Lige stepped outside, absently looking at the ground where Hamp had walked. There in the dusty street was the perfect outline of a boot print. For a moment, Lige didn't fully realize what he saw. He blinked and sucked in a hard breath.

Duncan joined him, and Lige said in a low, urgent voice, "Look at that, Cass."

Duncan's eyes followed Lige's pointing finger, and his face was puzzled. "I've seen footprints before," he said in sarcastic tones.

"Then you'd better take another look," Lige said. "You saw one just like it not too long ago."

Duncan's eyes widened as he bent over to examine the track. The dust was almost as good a mold as the dampened earth. There, clearly defined, was the outline of a boot sole, showing the hole in the middle and the run-over heel.

Duncan straightened, and a new glint appeared in his eyes. "Naw," he said incredulously. "It couldn't be. It don't come this easy."

Lige could appreciate how Duncan felt. He had known the same shocked disbelief when he first saw the track. The same print was repeated every other step. He nodded slowly. "That's the same track, Cass. Hamp killed Pancho."

He looked down the street. Hamp wasn't much more than a block ahead. "We can prove it one way or the other in a hurry," Lige said. He looked questioningly at Duncan.

Duncan's lips twisted in a semblance of a grin. "Did you think I was going to pass this up? We'd better talk to him."

Duncan lengthened his stride, and Lige had trouble keeping up with him. They caught up with Hamp before he had gone another block.

Hamp's eyes narrowed. He appeared shocked seeing Duncan and Lige together. He tried to grin, and the effort reminded Lige of a wolf baring its fangs.

"Well, if it ain't my little brother," Hamp said. "Oh, I forgot. You ain't my brother any more." He tried to talk naturally, but his tension was unmistakable.

"Better come with us, Hamp," Duncan said. His eyes were cold and remote.

"What for?" Hamp blustered. "I sure got no desire to see him again." He jerked his head at Lige.

"Come on down to the office, Hamp," Duncan said. He saw Hamp's stiffening and warned, "Any way you want it, Hamp. Hard or easy."

Hamp evaluated the two tense figures before him. "You got no right to arrest me. I ain't done nothing."

"Did I say anything about arresting you?" Duncan purred. "I just want to talk. You coming or not?"

Hamp's eyes swept from Duncan to Lige. Both of them

had the same watchful attitude. Hamp wore a gun, but he knew if he tried to touch it, he was a dead man.

His laugh had a false ring. "I don't know what the hell you have in mind. But if you want it that way, all right. But you're going to hear more about this."

"I expect to," Duncan returned. "Move!" The command had a new snap to it.

Hamp turned and went down the street, Duncan and Lige right behind him.

Hamp whirled as he stepped into Duncan's office. "Now, you tell me what this is all about."

Duncan closed the door and advanced toward Hamp. "Lay your gun on the desk, Hamp. Easy," he cautioned.

Hamp locked eyes with Duncan. The wildness in his eyes grew, and for a moment, Lige thought he was going to refuse.

"Sure," Hamp said and tried to laugh. "I don't know what this is all about, but I tell you one thing. Travis ain't going to like it."

"Pick up his gun, Lige," Duncan ordered. He waited until Lige picked up Hamp's gun. "I don't imagine he will, Hamp. Empty your pockets."

Hamp's eyes darted from face to face. Lige had the feeling he was looking at a trapped wild animal, desperately seeking a way to break free.

Hamp sullenly emptied his pockets on the desk. "By God," he threatened, "I'm not taking this kindly."

"Remind me to worry about that," Duncan jeered. He looked at the assorted items on the desk, a handful of change, a sack of tobacco and papers, and a horseshoe nail. His eyes had the gleam of winter ice as he looked at the wadded-up handkerchief.

"Do you see anything, Lige?" Duncan asked softly.

"Everything," Lige replied. Rage swept over him. He wanted to leap at Hamp and batter him into a pulp.

Duncan's eyes warned Lige not to do anything foolish, and Lige subsided, breathing hard.

"Let's see what he's got in there, Lige," Duncan suggested.

Lige's hands shook as he opened up the handkerchief. He knew what it held. He had seen that handkerchief before.

The silver of the bracelet reflected dull rays of light.

"Yes," Lige said. He couldn't trust himself to say more.

"That's an odd thing for a man to be carrying around," Duncan said. "Where did you get that bracelet, Hamp?"

Hamp's eyes were harried, and sweat broke out on his forehead. He looked as though he was trapped and really couldn't say why.

"It's mine," he said sullenly. "Is there any law against a man carrying a bracelet in his pocket?" His eyes flicked from one face to the other, though they couldn't remain long on either one. He was visibly trembling, and the sweating had increased. "Why are you looking at me like that?" he yelled.

"There may be a law against you carrying that particular bracelet, Hamp," Duncan said softly.

Hamp was breaking before the force of those cold, accusing eyes. "You just tell me one reason why you're holding me." Hamp's voice kept rising until it threatened to break.

"Try murder for a start." Duncan's face turned raw and savage. "Get on back to that cell." At Hamp's hesitation, Duncan yelled, "Damned if I wouldn't like to see you resist."

All of Hamp's resistance melted. He turned and stumbled toward the cell Duncan indicated. Duncan gave him a final shove that sent him reeling into the cell. Duncan slammed the door, and Lige heard the metallic click as Duncan turned the key.

Duncan came back to Lige, Hamp's yelling following him all the way.

"Have you got enough on him, Cass?" Lige asked.

"More than enough," Duncan answered. He stared at Lige. "What makes you ask that?"

"I was thinking of a jury in this county. Give them half a chance, and a jury will turn him loose."

"They won't get that half chance," Duncan said grimly.

"Not with the evidence I have." He hesitated a moment, then said, "I'll need your testimony, Lige." He looked curiously at Lige. "Does that bother you?"

Lige drew a long breath as he visualized a packed courtroom. The waves of hostility would hit him with a tangible force.

"It doesn't bother me," he said steadily. "Nothing could keep me from testifying."

"Thought you'd feel that way," Duncan said with satisfaction. "I don't think Judge Hacker is busy tomorrow. He hates a murderer as much as I do."

"I'll be there," Lige said. He walked toward the door. Denvers and Lisa had followed Lige into town. He had to tell them about this new happening. Then there was Pancho's funeral to attend. Lige sighed. This day had sure turned into a harried one.

CHAPTER EIGHTEEN

The courtroom was overflowing when Lige came in with Denvers and Lisa the next morning. People stood against the walls on both sides and in the back, though there were a few empty chairs in the first row.

Lige paused uncertainly. Should he proceed to the empty chairs, or would the standing people object?

Duncan was sitting on the front row. He looked around at Lige and nodded.

Lige bobbed his head in return. He supposed he could thank Duncan for those empty chairs. He guessed Duncan wanted his star witness near the bench.

Lige followed Denvers and Lisa down the narrow aisle. My God, she walks like a queen, he thought admiringly. Her head was high, her shoulders squared. She seemed completely oblivious to the whispers following her passage. The jury members craned their necks to watch her. Lisa was a good-looking woman, but there was no appreciation on the faces of the watchers.

Lige studied the jury as he sat down. Their attitude was a solid indication as to the general feeling in this room. He knew every one of those jurors. Half of them were merchants, the rest were cattlemen. The fact that not a single sheepman had been selected was indicative of the general feeling of animosity. The merchants might listen to the evidence against Hamp, but Lige could bet the cattlemen would close their ears. He was getting angry all over again just thinking of how unfair this trial could be.

Lige transferred his attention to Judge Hacker, sitting on the bench. The judge was heavy-eyed, looking almost sleepy. A casual observer would swear this judge wouldn't hear half of the evidence. Lige knew how wrong that would be. Judge Hacker had a mind as sharp as a newly honed knife, and those blue eyes could blaze when he looked at an offender.

Lige looked at Ben Samualson, the prosecuting attorney. Samualson was small, almost frail, and with that bald head he looked completely harmless and incompetent. But Samualson had the instincts of a rat terrier in pursuit of a rodent. Lige had talked to him an hour earlier this morning. Samualson had nodded repeatedly as he listened to Lige. He sensed Lige's doubt, for his final words were, "Quit worrying about it, Lige. I'll get a conviction."

Lige's doubts returned stronger than ever as he felt the hostility in the room. The attitude was as overpowering as a mule's kick. Nobody was going to convict Hamp Matlock of the murder of a sheepherder.

Lige glanced at the other table before the bench. Hamp and Willie Ulman sat there. Ulman was a big, hearty man with an unruly shock of white hair. He kept tossing that mane out of his eyes. Hamp whispered something to him and snickered. Ulman tossed back his hair again and laughed boisterously. Even Judge Hacker's glare didn't faze him.

Lige was looking at a man who was confident he would win his case. Why shouldn't he feel that way? Lige groaned silently. Ulman might have the judge against him, but he had the jury on his side. It was written all over their faces, and that was more important to Ulman.

The clerk read the charges against Hamp Matlock: murder of one Pancho Fernández.

Lige realized he had never heard Pancho's last name.

"How do you plead?" the judge asked icily.

"Why, not guilty, your honor," Ulman's big voice boomed out. "Hell, Judge, how could he be? He was—"

Hacker cut Ulman short with a furious banging of his gavel. "That's enough, Mr. Ulman," he snapped. "That's why this trial is being held—to establish your client's innocence or guilt."

Ulman looked at the jury and shrugged before he sat down. The gesture was more eloquent than any words. It said plainly, what are you going to do with a thick-headed judge?

Samualson called Duncan as his first witness. "You were out to the scene, Sheriff?" he asked softly.

"I was," Duncan said crisply.

"Describe what you saw, Sheriff."

In dispassionate tones, Duncan related what he found. His delivery was more effective than if he had shouted. He told of the slaughtered sheep, of the utter brutality of the act. "I'd say dynamite was used, to kill as many animals as I saw."

Ulman was on his feet. "Objection," he yelled.

Judge Hacker looked questioningly at him.

"I don't think the jury is interested in a few dead sheep," Ulman said.

"Overruled," Hacker snapped. "I think the killing of the sheep is an integral part of this trial."

Ulman looked at the jury again and shrugged helplessly. Lige heard the snickers run through the room. It sounded to him as though everybody in this room was solidly behind Ulman. Lige looked at his hands. They were tightly clenched in his lap. This is only the beginning, he told himself. But that damned Ulman was skillfully molding public opinion in favor of Hamp. Lige hadn't taken time to pick out Travis and Ordie as he entered the room, but he had no doubt they were here. How they must be enjoying this.

"You found a man shot, Sheriff," Samualson prompted.

Duncan nodded. "Pancho Fernández was lying at the bottom of the steps to his wagon. He had been shot twice."

Duncan's version was just fine with Lige. Lige was the one who found Pancho, but if the jury chose to believe that it had been the sheriff, Lige thought that was all to the good.

"Go on, Sheriff," Samualson murmured.

"Evidently, Pancho came out of his wagon to help his

dog. The dog had been poisoned and crawled up to the wagon. Pancho was shot then."

"Ah," Samualson said thoughtfully. "You say the dog was poisoned. Are you certain of that?"

"As near as I can be," Duncan replied impatiently. "The dog's lips were drawn back, and there was dried foam on its jaws. I've seen poisoned animals before."

"Objection," Ulman bellowed. "The sheriff is not a veterinarian. He isn't capable of drawing such a conclusion."

Judge Hacker nodded. "Sustained."

Samualson's eyebrows rose, but he made no further argument. He turned back to Duncan. "You think someone poisoned the dog to draw Pancho from his wagon."

"I couldn't be more positive," Duncan said flatly.

"How can you be so positive?" Samualson asked.

"By the footprints around the wagon. The murderer left a very distinctive footprint."

Ulman stared intently at Duncan. This was taking a turn he didn't like.

"What was so distinctive about those footprints?" Samualson pressed on.

"The man who wore those boots had a hole in the sole of his left boot, and the heel was badly run over."

"Ah," Samualson said again. "Do you know the man who wore that boot?"

"I do. It was Hamp Matlock."

"Objection," Ulman roared at the top of his voice. "What kind of a magician do we have here? He can look at a footprint and tell who made it. Why damn it—"

Hacker banged furiously with his gavel. "That's enough," he barked, cutting Ulman short.

Ulman wilted under the glare of those fierce old eyes.

"Objection is sustained. Unless Sheriff Duncan can prove he has powers beyond those of an ordinary man." Hacker glanced questioningly at Samualson.

"No further questions, your honor," Samualson said smoothly. "I call Hamp Matlock as my next witness."

Hamp's face showed his worry as he took the chair and sat down.

Lige thought he glanced furtively at his left boot.

"Were you out at the scene of the murder two nights before, Mr. Matlock?" Samualson asked.

"Hell no," Hamp said indignantly. "I was home all night. Travis and Ordie will tell you that."

Samualson sprang to the attack. "I'm asking *you*," he snapped.

"I've already told you," Hamp said sullenly.

Samualson thrust the bracelet at him. "Do you recognize this?"

Hamp looked uneasily at Ulman. Ulman shook his head, worry showing in the gesture. He didn't know where this questioning was going.

"Answer me," Samualson snapped.

Hamp's face was getting redder, and he began to squirm. "All right," he shouted. "It's mine. I picked it up for my girl. I never heard of any law that says a man can't do that."

"Certainly not," Samualson murmured. He walked a few steps away from Hamp, then whirled on him. "Mr. Matlock, show us the sole of your left boot."

Hamp stared defiantly at Samualson until Hacker said, "Obey him, Mr. Matlock."

Hamp reluctantly lifted his left foot, holding the leg out before him.

He started to lower the leg, and Samualson said almost pleasantly, "Hold it up. All of us want to see that boot sole." He placed both hands under Hamp's ankle to help him hold up the boot.

"Can everybody see this?" Samualson asked. He turned Hamp's foot in the direction of the jury, and Hamp had to twist in his chair to follow the pressure Samualson exerted on his foot.

"This is most interesting," Samualson remarked. "A hole in the sole and a run-over heel. This boot could make the exact footprint Sheriff Duncan described."

A stunned silence fell over the room, then voices broke

out in excited talk. The jurors had their heads together, talking among themselves.

It took more furious pounding for Hacker to restore quiet in the room. "I demand order," he said coldly when he could finally be heard. "Another outbreak like this, and I'll hold every person in this room in contempt of court."

Ulman struggled to his feet, screaming objection. His face was as red as Hamp's. Samualson had boxed him in, and he knew it.

"Of all the goddamned nonsense," he spluttered. "Because a man has a hole in the sole of his boot, Mr. Samualson"—Ulman stopped long enough to sneer at his opponent—"is accusing my client of murder. Why hell. In a half day's time, I could find fifty men with similar holes in their boots." He stabbed a finger at Samualson. "And on such flimsy evidence, he accuses my client of murder."

Hacker had risen from his chair and was leaning forward, his face wrathful. "Have you finished trying your case, Mr. Ulman? Because one more word out of you is going to cost you twenty-five dollars."

"Yes, sir," Ulman said weakly and sank into his chair. But he was grinning broadly. He had knocked down every point Samualson had made.

Samualson's smile had a wolfish cast. "That'll be all, Mr. Matlock. I call my next witness. Lige Madison."

Lige rose and approached the witness chair. He sat down, facing the room. How many times had he told himself that this wasn't going to bother him, but he was so tight he ached. He couldn't believe that so much hostility had a physical force. He could feel all those eyes pouring out hatred at him.

"You've changed your name, Mr. Madison?" Samualson said.

Lige shook his head. "No, that is my real name. I was never a Matlock." Lige's eyes swept the room. Yes, Travis and Ordie were in the room, sitting next to Harley Inman. Travis was choking as though he was trying to swallow something too big to go down.

Lige's face was impassive as he heard the whispered speculation run through the room. Earlier this morning, he had told Samualson all about the name change, and Samualson had agreed it wasn't important. Lige hoped the lawyer didn't change his mind.

"What is your occupation, Mr. Madison?" Samualson asked.

A small sigh escaped Lige. Samualson was living up to his agreement; he wasn't delving into the name change further.

"I work for Cleve Denvers," Lige said steadily.

"My God," Ulman said in mock astonishment. "An admitted turncoat, and he goes to work for a sheepherder."

"Twenty-five dollars, Mr. Ulman," Hacker said grimly. "I warned you."

Ulman's face was flushed, but it didn't erase his triumph. He had established with the jury just what Lige was.

"What is your work, Mr. Madison?"

Lige gestured vaguely. "Mostly driving supplies out to the sheep camps. Anything else that needs to be done."

"Then you knew Pancho Fernández?"

Lige nodded. "Very well. We had long talks together."

Samualson picked up the bracelet. "Did he ever mention this?"

"Yes," Lige replied. "He bought it as a present for his wife." Briefly, Lige related the conversation with Pancho. "It was the last tie he had with her. She was killed in a raid on his sheep ranch, down in Arizona. That's why he came to Wyoming. To get away from his bad memories."

Again, a stunned silence held the room, then a babble of excited talk broke out. Hacker gaveled furiously before he could restore order to the room.

Samualson held the bracelet higher. "Pancho wouldn't have parted with this?"

"No," Lige said firmly. "There was only one way for anybody to get it. A man would have to kill Pancho to get that bracelet."

Ulman bounded to his feet, screaming objection at the top of his lungs.

Hacker glared at him until Ulman was quiet. "What is your objection, Mr. Ulman?" he asked in a frosty tone.

"Pure conjecture on the witness's part," Ulman stated. "Mr. Madison had no way of knowing what Pancho Fernández would do under any set of circumstances."

Hacker considered Ulman's objection, then nodded. "Sustained," he said.

Lige glanced at Hamp. Hamp's face was white, and his mouth worked. Lige was surprised Hamp didn't break under the direct accusation, but Hamp stared directly ahead. Lige could see Hamp's hands in his lap. They were clenched tight, the knuckles standing out starkly. Hell yes, Hamp was guilty. Lige hadn't had any doubt of it from the start. He wouldn't be surprised that everybody in the room had reached the same conclusion, but the big problem was, had the law reached that conclusion?

Samualson had been watching Hamp with the same intensity, and Lige thought he saw his shoulders droop. No, it wasn't an actual physical movement; it was more of a sagging of the spirit. Lige thought with keen perception that Samualson had expected Hamp to break under proof of his guilt, and it hadn't happened.

"Mr. Madison," Samualson asked, "in your opinion, do you think—" He smiled bleakly and said, "Never mind. You can step down, Mr. Madison. I have no more witnesses, your honor."

Ulman and Hamp had their heads together, conferring in hushed tones. At Hacker's pounding, Ulman looked up and said, "Just another moment, your honor."

The moment stretched out, and by the increasing color in the judge's face, Lige knew Hacker's temper was wearing thin.

Ulman stood and said, "I am ready now, your honor. I call as my first witness Hamp Matlock."

Samualson never took his eyes off of Hamp. Lige could swear that Samualson was so tight that he would twang if he were plucked. Somehow Lige knew Samualson's case would be won or lost in the next few moments.

Duncan had the same worried, intense look on his face. He, too, knew Samualson's case teetered on a thin edge.

"Hamp," Ulman said cheerfully, "you've seen this bracelet before, haven't you?"

"You mean before I bought it?" Hamp asked. His breathing had almost returned to normal, and that tight, pinched look was gone from his lips. "I saw a dozen just like it when I bought this one."

"A dozen?" Ulman asked in mock astonishment.

Hamp nodded. "Sure. From a peddler. That's why he made me such a good price on this one. He told me they were genuine Indian work. From the number the peddler had, the Indian oversold him. That peddler was sure anxious to get rid of them."

"Do you know the peddler's name?" Ulman asked.

Hamp snorted. "Who pays any attention to these wandering peddlers. I never saw him before or since."

"Did anybody see you buy this bracelet from the peddler?" Ulman asked.

Hamp rubbed his forehead as he scowled. His face cleared, and he shouted, "Hell yes. Travis and Ordie came into the barn while that peddler was there. Travis raised hell about me buying a trinket."

Hamp's words released excited talk all over the room. Lige thought Hacker was going to break his gavel.

"This is the last time I warn you," Hacker said, breathing hard. "One more outbreak and this room will be cleared." He glared about him and demanded, "Is that understood?"

He was satisfied with the following silence, for he said, "Proceed, Mr. Ulman."

Lige saw physical evidence of Samualson's defeat, for his shoulders slumped. Samualson had enough experience to know how that jury would take this testimony.

Travis took the chair and nodded vigorously to Ulman's questions. "Sure, I saw Hamp buy that bracelet from the peddler. I cussed him out good for wasting his money on such cheap stuff. But you know how young'uns are." He shrugged and grinned at the jury.

Liar, Lige wanted to scream at him. He kept his face stolid, but he knew how this verdict was going. He could tell by the loosening of the jurors' faces. A moment ago, these faces had been tight and worried.

Ordie repeated Travis's story almost word for word.

Both of them are accomplished liars, Lige thought savagely. He didn't dare look at Lisa or Denvers.

"I rest my case, your honor," Ulman said.

Oh God, Lige thought. If only he could get up and smash the smugness off of Ulman's face. He knew what the verdict would be before the jury came back into the courtroom.

The jury wasn't out thirty minutes. A little hope remained in Lige until the last second. Surely, some of them had enough sense to see this pack of trumped-up lies.

The jury filed back into the room, and Childers, the foreman, said, "We find Hamp Matlock not guilty, your honor."

Judge Hacker closed his eyes as though he was suddenly weary. When he reopened them, they were empty. "I have the feeling we have just witnessed a grave miscarriage of justice," he said tonelessly. "Sheriff, you will release your prisoner."

The judge rose, and some of the old blaze returned to his eyes. "This should frighten every sane man who saw it," he said. He leveled a finger as though he was accusing every person in this room. "These outrages will stop. I promise you I will do everything in my power to prevent this from happening again." He turned and left the room through a rear door.

Samualson clasped Lige's shoulders briefly, nodded to him, and pushed his way through the crowd in the courtroom.

"He feels as bad as I do," Duncan said moodily. "I saw and heard it, but by God, I still don't believe it. I was so damned positive we'd finally caught up with one of the sneaking murderers. Look at them!" He swept his arm about at the people in the room.

It wasn't hard to understand Duncan's bitterness. People were pumping hands and congratulating each other.

Duncan's face twisted with rage and disgust. "They act as though they'd won a victory. The damned fools. Don't they realize they've just seen justice break down?"

He made a tremendous effort and calmed himself. "Lige, get Denvers and Lisa out of town as fast as you can. I wish Harper and I could go with you, but there's no telling what this crazy town will do tonight."

"Sure, Cass," Lige said in quick understanding. He had marked himself openly as a sheepman. As enflamed as this town was, there was no telling what it would do next.

"What do you expect, Cass?" he asked quietly.

"I don't know what to expect next," Duncan said heavily. "Watch yourself good, Lige. The Matlocks know where you are now."

Lige was tight-lipped as he nodded. He didn't need Duncan's warning to be told how vengeful the Matlocks were.

"We'll get out of town right now, Cass," he said.

CHAPTER NINETEEN

Every man who passed the Matlocks' table offered to buy them another drink. Hamp's flushed face showed how many of those offers he had accepted.

"Better slow down, Hamp," Travis growled, "or we'll be carrying you out of here."

"Damn it," Hamp said indignantly, "if this ain't a day to celebrate, I don't know what is. I'm telling you I felt a rope around my neck when Lige described where he'd seen that bracelet before."

He paused to accept another group's congratulations.

"You really showed them, Hamp," one of them said. "Who would've thunk your own brother would have turned against you that way?" The speaker's face turned florid under his outrage. "Why, by God, he could've got you hung."

"Don't I know that," Hamp said fervently. He turned down the offer of more free drinks. "I'm holding off for a few minutes," he said and grinned.

The four men who had approached him stood around for a moment longer. "That should've set back that smart-assed Duncan," one of them said. "He knew damned well there was no evidence that would make a charge of murder against you stand up." The man shook his head in amazement. "Damned if I would've believed Duncan was so one-sided. This sure shows he stands on the sheepmen's side, don't it?"

"It does," Hamp said gravely. "Thanks for the offers and good wishes, boys."

He waited until the four left before he said, "They were

right about Duncan, weren't they? But I sure whittled some of his ass off, didn't I?"

"Listen to him," Ordie jeered. "As usual, he's grabbing for all the credit. Hamp, you never could think fast enough to get out of the bind you were in. I was watching you. I swear you turned green."

Hamp's face flamed. "You shut your mouth," he said belligerently. "I told Ulman what to say to get me out of it."

Ordie hooted in derision. "Pa, would you listen to that. Don't try to lie to us, Hamp. I saw how you looked before Ulman told you something. You changed completely then. Don't brag to me about how smart you are. In the first place, I wouldn't have been stupid enough to pick up that bracelet. That's what nailed you." He was getting through to Hamp, and his triumph shone from his face. "Ulman put that story into your head. What would you have done if Travis and I hadn't backed up your story about that peddler?"

Travis grinned maliciously at Hamp's discomfort. "He's got you, Hamp, and you know it. I'm a little curious myself. What would you have done, if Ordie and me dropped out from under you?"

Hamp swallowed hard. "I'd be in a fix, Pa," he said honestly. "That jury would've hung me sure as hell. That goddamned Lige," he said passionately. "Wait until I get my hands on him."

"I suppose you want to go out looking for him now," Travis said in a caustic voice.

"You're damned right I do," Hamp snapped.

"That'd be real smart, wouldn't it?" Travis demanded. "You wait until I round up Duncan so he can watch you kill Lige." He shook his head in utter disgust. "I never saw no one so determined to get himself hung."

Hamp squirmed. "You don't think I'm going to let what Lige did pass, do you, Pa? He's the one who dug that hole for me, then shoved me into it."

Travis's eyes were mean in a squinched-up face. "You didn't hear me say anything like that, did you, Hamp? Hell no, Lige's gonna pay for the worry he put us through. But jumping him right here in town ain't the answer. We'll let things simmer down a few days before we move." His temper rose at the disappointment flooding Hamp's face. "Will it hurt you to wait a few days? We know where he is now, don't we? We can reach out and pick him off any time we choose."

Hamp's face brightened. "You're right, Pa. We know where he is. It's gonna be hard to wait, but we can go after him any time you want to."

Travis looked around the noisy, crowded room. "Where's that damned Inman? He promised me he'd join us here."

Hamp didn't have much use for Harley Inman. The man's bossy manner got on his nerves. "Suits me just as well if he never shows up again," he grumbled.

"When will you start using your head, Hamp?" Travis asked in disgust. "Harley has as much reason to hate Lige as we do. Can't you see?" he asked in exasperation. "Every time Harley looks at Stobie, he remembers Lige. Would it do any harm to have a little help along with us?"

Hamp grinned. "I guess you're right, Pa. It would do no harm at all."

Travis looked toward the door again. "Ah," he said with satisfaction in his voice. "Here comes Harley now."

CHAPTER TWENTY

Lige and Denvers spent two hard days digging the remains of Pancho's flock out of the brush. The physical exertion was the least of the drain; the effect was far worse on mind and spirit.

Only once had the subject of the trial come up. "There's no goddamned justice in this country," Denvers burst out.

"You can't allow yourself to believe that, Cleve," Lige said evenly.

Duncan turned a twisted face toward him. "You can say that after what you saw?" he asked bitterly. "I tell you there's no hope left."

Lige shook his head. He sympathized with everything Denvers said, but a man couldn't allow himself to dwell on that line. "Without that hope, Cleve, you might as well be dead."

"Don't give me any of that crap," Denvers yelled at him.

The subject wasn't brought up again, and Lige was just as content that it was so. Words wouldn't lift Denvers out of the depression he felt.

Hourly, Lige saw the strain digging deeper lines into Denvers' face. Everything they found only increased the strain. It was damned hard to shoot a wounded ewe; it was even harder to shoot her lamb, but it had to be done.

Lige recalled how Denvers sounded as he shot the first sheep. "She had one chance out of a thousand to make it, Lige. There's no way of taking care of her lamb."

Lige's lips were a thin line as he nodded. This was a horrible thing, for a man to have to destroy his own stock. The orphaned lambs whose mothers died in the dynamite blast received the same treatment.

The predators had taken further toll of the remaining un-guarded sheep. Lige could imagine the anguish Denvers suffered each time they found such a mutilated animal. But Denvers merely clamped his lips more tightly together and plowed ahead, looking for more sheep, dead or alive.

Lige thought he had disliked Hamp before. I was wrong, he thought, as he walked along. He now knew a deep hatred that even appalled him. Lige was going to see Hamp Matlock again; that was inevitable. When that happened, there wouldn't be the slightest hesitation about what he would do. A man who had handed out as much misery as Hamp had didn't deserve the slightest consideration.

Stop clubbing yourself with such thinking, Lige rebuked himself. Forget it until the time comes to wipe it all out.

Denvers worked his way through a thicket and rejoined Lige. "Found two more sheep, Lige," he said dejectedly. "Coyotes or wolves got them."

Lige looked at the sun. It was getting well on into the af-ternoon. "Do you think there's any more, Cleve?"

"Maybe," Denvers answered. "But there won't be enough to make it worth while spending any more time looking for them."

Lige looked at the small flock of sheep they had gathered. "How many do you figure you lost?"

Denvers gestured savagely at the sheep. "We've got a few head over six hundred. There were two thousand head in Pancho's stock when he was killed. Figure it out for your-self."

Lige whistled. Between the dynamite and the predators, Denvers had suffered a grievous loss. "What are you going to do now, Cleve?"

Denvers stared at him with surprise. "Why, take these sheep home," he said in a matter-of-fact tone. "If you think this is going to force me to quit, you couldn't be more wrong. I've had losses before. I've worked out of them."

"Sure," Lige replied. He knew Denvers better than to think this loss would drive him out of business. Denvers was tougher than that.

Neither of them spoke much on the way home. Lige asked about Pancho's wagon, and Denvers replied irritably, "We'll come back and get it tomorrow." He sounded as though he didn't want to be reminded of any part of this sorry event.

A horse was ground-reined before the house, and in the approaching darkness, Lige didn't recognize the animal. "Looks like we've got a visitor," he said, his voice tighter than he intended. Any lone rider was suspect until he was identified. "Cleve, go ahead and see who it is. I'll build a corral for the sheep."

Denvers wavered in indecision. "Maybe I'd better find out," he muttered.

Lige knew Denvers couldn't relax until he found out who the visitor was.

"I'll be back and help you," Denvers said. "There's some muslin with the stakes already attached in the shed."

Lige nodded and walked into the shed. He found the rolls with no trouble. It wouldn't take much work to build a corral for this small bunch of sheep.

Lige had just started unrolling the muslin when Denvers returned. "It's Duncan," he announced. "He's drinking coffee with Lisa."

Lige caught the strain in Denver's voice. "More bad news?"

"He said it was just a visit to see that everything was going all right, but I think he's holding something back. Probably didn't want to alarm Lisa. He said he'd be right out."

Duncan joined them just as the last sheep was driven into the corral.

"That's all that's left?" Duncan asked. He tried to make the question too casual.

"All right, Cass," Lige said evenly. "What is it?"

"No more trouble," Duncan said gruffly. "I just came out to see how you two are getting along."

"We're getting along just fine," Denvers said bitterly. "Of course, that's not considering that I lost more than I can make back in several years. I sat in that courtroom and watched the man responsible smirk all over his face when that goddamned jury freed him."

Lige touched Denvers on the arm, not so much to restrain him, for God knew Denvers had earned his right to this tirade, but more to tell him this wouldn't accomplish a thing.

Denvers flashed Lige a searing look, then appeared to wilt spiritually.

"I wasn't blaming you, Cass," Denvers said dully. "But sometimes it gets more than a man can bear."

Duncan nodded without speaking. The muted gesture said Denvers had all his sympathy.

"The town's quieter," he said. "Though I'm still afraid trouble can break out again. I left Harper there to keep his eyes open, but I feel I should get back as soon as I can."

"But you had a special reason to come by here?" Lige asked quietly.

"No," Duncan said harshly. "Hamp came too close to hanging, but he's too thick-headed to see that. It's enough to make a sane man run for cover. But all Hamp will be able to see is getting even. He won't blame himself for being tried. He'll blame you for pointing a finger at him and putting him there."

Duncan's words sent an icy tremor down Lige's spine. "That doesn't help much now, does it, Cass?" he asked wryly.

"Lige, why don't you come into town with me? That way, I could keep an eye on you."

The offer was momentarily tempting, then Lige shook his head. "That only takes care of a few days, Cass. You can't watch me for the rest of my life, can you?" He grinned wanly at Duncan's gloomy expression. It told Lige that he had scored. He clenched his argument by saying, "There's no way I would leave Cleve and Lisa out here alone."

Duncan sighed. "I knew you'd see it that way." He sought for a final bolstering of his argument. "Inman and Travis both have every reason to hate you. You shot Stobie, and your testimony in court almost nailed down Hamp. Neither of them can forgive or forget, Lige."

"They can't," Lige agreed. Travis and Inman were vindictive men.

Duncan stared at him, then said, "I've racked my brain trying to find some way to stop what I know is going to happen. I even thought of arresting Inman and Travis and throwing them into jail. But that wouldn't do any good," he finished wearily. "I could only hold them so long on suspicion." He sounded like a man up against a wall with no way through it. "The minute they got out they'd only pick up where they left off."

Lige spit on the ground. "I can understand that, Cass. Quit fretting about it."

Duncan muttered an oath, turned, and strode toward his horse.

Denvers and Lige waited until the echoes of horse hoofs faded away.

"We'd better go in, Cleve," Lige suggested.

Denvers shivered as though a cold wind had suddenly buffeted him. "Yeah," he said. "I feel kinda naked, standing out here."

"We've got to talk, Cleve," Lige said as he started for the house.

Denvers caught up with him. "Go ahead. Talk!"

"In a moment," Lige said. He wanted Lisa to hear what he had to say. That was her right; she was involved in this, too.

Lisa was waiting for them at the door. Her eyes swept their faces.

"More trouble?" she asked, her voice tight.

"What did Duncan tell you?" Lige asked in a cautious tone.

"He praised my coffee. Drank three cups of it," she replied tartly. "But he kept asking me if I thought you two would get here soon. Damn it, Lige. Don't you think I have the right to know what's going on?"

Lige looked at those blazing eyes in a taut face. Lisa's toughness was showing again.

"Yes," he said. "I think you have." He drew a deep breath

before he sat down. "Cass feels sure Travis and Inman will be coming after me. He named a couple of solid reasons why they should."

Lisa's eyes never left Lige's face. "Do you think they will?" she asked bluntly.

"It figures," Lige said in a quiet voice.

At his silence, Lisa said fiercely, "Go on."

"I don't want to bring any more trouble on you two," Lige replied. "I'm thinking of riding out."

That really hit Lisa wrong, and Lige was awed by the fury in her eyes.

"Do you think that would do any good?" Denvers asked morosely.

Lisa was far more positive. "You will not," she said vehemently. "All of us are in this together. We'll wait and see what happens." The blaze faded from her eyes. "Can't you see, Lige? You didn't bring trouble on us. You've only helped us to meet it."

Lige looked searchingly at Lisa and felt as though he was melting inside. All he had to go on was the unspoken promise behind those lovely eyes, but it was enough.

He looked squarely at Denvers. "Is that the way you feel?" he asked.

"She said it better than I could," Denvers said crossly. "How about supper? My belly is growling."

"Are you going to blame that on me?" Lisa retorted with a flash of the old spirit. "How did I know when to have supper ready?"

Denvers gave Lige a strained smile. "Don't know what I'm going to do with her. The older she gets, the sassier she gets."

Lige's eyes kept straying to Lisa as she went about preparing supper. Each time, he found Denvers looking at him. There was a tightness about Denver's mouth that troubled Lige.

He knows how I feel, Lige thought. Maybe he sees the same feeling in Lisa. It was a big mouthful, and Denvers was having difficulty swallowing it.

CHAPTER TWENTY-ONE

Hamp answered the knock on the kitchen door and said, "Hello, Harley." From the expression on his face, Inman had something heavy on his mind.

"Have a drink, Harley?" Travis offered.

Inman swept the invitation aside with a savage gesture. "This ain't no social visit." He looked from Hamp to Ordie to Travis. "Though it looks like the three of you are settled in for another comfortable evening."

Travis tried to meet the blaze in Inman's eyes and failed. "What's that supposed to mean?"

Inman breathed hard in an effort to control himself. "It's been a full three days since Hamp's trial. The way I heard you three say it, you couldn't wait to get at Lige. Maybe you didn't mean this year," he finished sarcastically.

Travis's face burned a bright red. "Don't go taking that hard line with me, Harley."

"I thought sure you'd be by my place last night." Inman's seething eyes swept them again. "I see I was wrong. And by the looks of you, you have no intention of going out to-night."

Travis stood, and his face worked. "Just a damned minute, Harley," he said heatedly. "I'm just making sure Duncan isn't poking his nose around." The color in his face showed how worked up he was.

"You don't have to worry about that tonight," Inman snapped. "I left town not an hour ago. Duncan and Harper had their hands full, quieting down a new brawl between sheepmen and cattlemen." He bared his teeth as he grinned. "I bought a lot of whiskey getting the cattlemen primed.

It's going to take Duncan most of the evening getting that brawl quieted down."

Inman enjoyed watching Travis squirm. "That takes away your last excuse, doesn't it, Travis? Unless you've given up the whole idea."

That stung Travis hard. "I'm not giving up on anything," he flared.

"Pa," Hamp said, "I've been after you to get moving. Looks like Harley's fixed up everything pretty good for us."

"Listen to him," Inman said in approval. "Sounds to me like Hamp's got all the backbone in this family."

Travis's nostrils pinched together with the rush of his breathing. "Don't say any more," he warned. He walked to the gun rack on the kitchen wall. He picked out a rifle and squinted down the barrel. "You ready to go now?" He glared at Inman.

"Barnes and Thomas are waiting at my place. They remember Lige shooting Stobie down, too. They want a piece of Lige's carcass."

"Gonna have to cut up that carcass pretty small," Travis grunted. He leaned the rifle against a wall, put on a jacket and dropped two boxes of shells into the pockets.

"Are you just going to sit there, Ordie?" Travis snarled. "Or do you figure you're safer here?"

Ordie ducked his head to keep the anger in his face hidden. "I'm coming, Pa," he said. "But I'd kinda like to know what we're heading into." He looked at Inman. He didn't have much use for the man. Ever since he had known Inman, he always ordered people around. "What if Lige doesn't come out?" he asked sullenly.

"You mean he'll refuse a polite invitation to come out?" Inman asked in mock amazement. The wildness returned to his face, and he raged, "Why, damn it, if he doesn't come out, we'll burn him out. Does that ease your worry, Ordie?" he sneered. "There'll be six of us. All Lige has with him is another sheepherder and that girl. You figure that's too many to go up against?"

Ordie's eyes smoldered. "I'm not worried," he said flatly.

He stormed mentally as he took his rifle out of the rack and dropped boxes of shells into his pocket. How in the hell did Inman get the reins in his hands? Inman ordered, and the Matlocks jumped. Some day, that was going to be changed.

"How come you didn't know Lige was working for Denvers?" Inman asked Travis pointedly as they walked outside.

"How could I?" Travis said defensively. "I thought he was clean out of the country. I never gave him another thought until I saw him in court." The memory of that day inflamed his face, and he said savagely, "Hell yes, I want to see him again. Just one more time. He almost got Hamp hanged."

Inman nodded as though he was satisfied. "I'll wait here," he said as he reached his horse, "while you get saddled up. The sooner we get this over, the better pleased I'll be." He paused in bitter reflection. "It's too bad Stobie can't go along and see this. He'll be a lot happier when I tell him it's done." He winked at Hamp. "I guess you're looking forward to the same thing."

"You can bet on that," Hamp said fiercely.

Travis grumbled about Inman all the way to the barn. "He gets on my nerves. He acts like he's got a bit in my mouth."

"I didn't think you noticed, Pa," Ordie said sardonically. He stepped quickly to one side as Travis's hand lifted. "Just funning, Pa," he said plaintively.

"You watch your damned mouth," Travis roared. "When this is over, I'm through with Harley Inman. All he's done for us is to get us in a fix."

He stepped inside the barn and yelled, "Brunner."

His face turned mean at the lack of response. "That worthless Brunner. All he's good for any more is to saddle the horses. And he's not around even for that."

Travis kept up his grumbling as he smoothed out the blanket on the horse's back. He grunted as he lifted his saddle from its bar. "Andy's in the same class as Lige," he said petulantly. "After tonight, if I fire Andy, I'll be rid of both of them."

Travis mounted, and his horse danced impatiently while Travis waited for Hamp and Ordie to finish saddling. "You two gonna take all night?" he yelled.

"We're coming, Pa," Hamp answered for both of them.

They joined Travis, and the three rode together toward the big barn door. Travis jerked hard on his reins as a figure materialized at his side.

To cover his start, Travis yelled, "Where in the hell have you been?"

"I got out here as fast as I could," Brunner said quietly. "Are you going after Lige now, Travis?"

The question took Travis by surprise, and it showed in the jerk of his head. "What makes you ask a damn fool question like that?"

"I saw Inman ride up," Brunner replied. "I know how he feels about Lige. I'd hoped it hadn't gone that far with you, yet."

Travis exploded. "You think I shouldn't," he said hotly. "After Lige lied about Hamp in court?"

Brunner shifted his weight. He looked squarely at Travis, but he didn't speak.

That accusing look was additional fuel to the fire burning within Travis. His face turned violent as a thought struck him.

"Did you know Lige was working for Denvers?"

"I knew," Brunner admitted. "I ran across him one day. I didn't see any reason to mention it to you."

Travis's fury choked him, and spittle ran down from a lip corner. "You knew and didn't come to me? Why, you sonovabitch. You could've kept Hamp out of a lot of trouble."

Travis jerked his boot out of the stirrup and kicked Brunner full in the face.

Brunner made a garbled sound of groans and words. He threw up his hands to retain his balance, but his legs buckled under him, and he went down in a crumpled heap.

Travis sawed on the reins to get his horse under control. "Hold it, you damned fool," he roared. He stopped the lunging and bucking, but the horse still danced nervously.

Travis looked down at the motionless figure. "I oughta kill you," he panted. "The only thing that saves you is what you once did for me." His voice rose until he was screaming. "You better be gone when I get back."

Travis's breathing was a hard, rasping sound as he whirled his horse and left the barn.

Hamp and Ordie caught up with him. "That's one way of getting rid of him, Pa," Hamp said and grinned.

Travis's eyes were murderous. "You keep your mouth shut. I don't want you blabbering any of this to Inman."

"Not me," Hamp said hastily. When Travis was in this mood, nobody was safe around him.

"You took long enough," Inman said as the three joined him. "Did I hear a ruckus at the barn?"

Travis glared at him. "I just fired a hand," he snapped.

"I'm glad to hear that," Inman said and grinned. "You know, Travis, you always did have too soft a streak for your own good."

Travis stared stonily ahead. He wasn't ready to admit anything to Inman, but Inman could be sure of one thing. There was no softness in him now.

Brunner made a third attempt before he managed to make it to his feet. He hadn't been unconscious, but God, his head roared, and he was sick to his stomach.

"All right, Travis," he muttered. "I'll get off your land." He raised a hand to his face, and even the light touch made him wince. He wasn't surprised to find the stickiness on his fingers. He was lucky to have a face left.

He gagged and spat out a mouthful of blood. He had trouble breathing, and his nose felt as though it was packed solid. He blew his nose, and the resulting pain made his head reel. At a touch, his nose wobbled from side to side under his fingers. He knew his nose was broken, and he was careful to make his breathing light and cautious. He didn't want that stabbing pain again.

Brunner leaned against a stall until his head cleared. "Travis," he muttered, "nobody kicks me in the face."

Brunner found he could walk if he took it slow and easy, but dear God, he was so weak, and his stomach heaved rebelliously before it finally settled down.

Saddling his horse took tremendous effort, and he stopped several times to wait until his strength returned.

"I'll be back," he said thickly to his horse and staggered out to the horse trough outside of the barn. He plunged his head into the water, holding it there until he was forced to lift it. The pain was still there, but his head was cleared.

He let the water run off his face before he reached for his handkerchief. But his head was back solidly on his shoulders, and he knew where he was going and what he had to do.

Brunner walked into the bunkhouse, rummaged in his war bag and pulled out his gun belt, and strapped it on. It had been a long time since he had worn a gun, and he wouldn't have believed the time would come when he wanted to use it against Travis Matlock. But that time had come.

He went back out to the barn and mounted, the effort making his stomach start heaving again. He thought he would vomit, and he sat there, his head hanging low until the nausea passed.

Brunner could join Lige, but he couldn't give Lige nearly enough help for what was going to hit him. He turned the horse toward town. "Let's go, boy," he muttered.

Duncan looked up as the bloody apparition staggered into his office. He stared hard before he recognized Brunner.

"My God, Andy," he cried, springing to his feet. He took hold of Brunner's arm and led him to a chair. "What happened to your face?"

"Travis and I had an argument," Brunner said dully. "He kicked me in the face."

Duncan swore in disbelief. "I'll get the Doc for you."

"There's no time for that," Brunner said wearily. His voice strengthened. "Travis and Inman are going to hit Denvers' place tonight. I don't know how far I am behind them."

Duncan's face was a chunk of ice; only the eyes held fire. "They'll never learn, will they?" he said. "I'll round up some men."

Brunner raised his head. "I told you there isn't much time."

"I heard you," Duncan snapped. "But I can't handle it by myself."

He started for the door, and Brunner said stubbornly, "I'm going too, Cass."

Duncan stopped and looked at him briefly. "I'd say you sure earned that right," he said.

CHAPTER TWENTY-TWO

Supper was over, and Lisa looked at the food remaining on the table. "Again, it looks as though I wasted my time." She tried to say it lightly, but there was a suspicious shakiness in her voice.

Lige laughed, hoping it rang true. "And again, I plead no appetite. You didn't do so well yourself. And look at Cleve. He hardly ate a mouthful."

Denvers shook his head without replying. He stared fixedly at the table, gloom pronounced on his face.

Lisa tried to return Lige's smile, and Lige thought, strain plays hell with a smile.

"I guess none of us is hungry," she said.

Silence fell again. Lige knew that Lisa and Denvers were thinking of Duncan's visit. The three of them had discussed the visit at length, and all that discussion hadn't solved a thing. Lige was weary of the subject, and he wanted to stop thinking and talking about it.

"Look!" he pointed out. "Nothing's happened yet, has it? Isn't there an old saying about crossing bridges?"

"Do you believe that?" Lisa challenged.

Lige sighed. He wasn't fooling her in the slightest. Hamp was a vindictive man, and he wouldn't stop until his distorted sense of satisfaction was appeased. Lige argued with this line of reasoning. Nothing had happened since the trial. Maybe Hamp had come so close to being convicted that it frightened him enough to make him leave the matter where it lay. But that was logical reasoning, and Lige had never known Hamp to be a logical man. The fact that Lige would have to face Hamp again didn't bother him. But the waiting; the letting Hamp pick the time was a hard thing to bear.

"What are you thinking about, Lige?" Lisa whispered.

Lige didn't try to avoid her eyes. There was no use trying to build false hope in her. She was too perceptive for that.

"I'm just thinking of getting through the night. One night at a time is all I can look at now." The tightness in her face distressed him. He sought for something assuring to say, anything to ease that tightness.

"I don't think anything's going to happen," Lige said. He prayed he was a convincing liar. "Hamp won't try anything." At least, not now, he thought. The look on her face said she didn't believe him any more than he believed himself.

He jumped as a rifle bullet ripped through the window. The pane was shattered, and the shade flopped. Lige thought he heard the thud of the slug hitting the opposite wall.

Lisa screamed, then pressed a tightly clenched fist against her mouth. Denvers sprang to his feet, overturning his chair. His eyes were wild and staring.

"Down," Lige yelled. He wished he could sweep the lamp off the table, but the fire danger was too great. He reached up from the floor and removed the globe from the lamp base. He winced at the hot pain in his fingers. He set the globe on the table and blew out the wick, then flattened out on the floor.

Lisa was beside him, and Lige heard her shallow breathing.

"It's started, Lige," she said in a small, frightened voice.

"Maybe that was just an accident. Somebody passing by and letting off an unaimed shot." Lige swore at himself for the unpalatable lie.

The following silence was overwhelming. Lige's eyes adjusted to the darkness, and he crawled over to the corner, where he left his rifle. Denvers found his rifle too, for Lige heard the sound of a shell being pumped into the chamber.

This was the real torment, the endless waiting. Why

didn't they go ahead and follow up what they started? Lige's skin felt too tight to contain his bones. At any second, he expected a fusillade of bullets to break out. What were they waiting for?

"Lige," a voice yelled, "do you hear me?"

That was Inman's voice, and Lige's rage dispelled some of the hard knot of fear in his belly. He saw no sense in not answering Inman. Inman knew he was here. The sudden extinguishing of the lamp was answer enough. Lige crawled to a window and raised himself enough so that he could cautiously lift a corner of the shade.

"You might as well come out," Hamp yelled.

Those voices sounded fairly close. Lige estimated Inman and Hamp were within two hundred yards of the house. He clutched his rifle so tightly that his hands ached. Oh God, if he could only catch a glimpse of them.

Lige saw no movement out there, and the night was too dark for him to pick out anything that he could distinguish as a human form. But every hump, every swag in the ground could easily hide a man.

"I hear you," Lige called back.

"You can come out and save Denvers and his daughter," Inman called back. "If we have to come in after you, I'm not promising you anything."

Lige looked helplessly at Denvers and Lisa. He could see only the pale ovals of their faces. He had tried to tell them this would happen, but they had refused to listen to him.

He cleared his throat, but before he could speak Denvers said fiercely, "Tell the lying bastard to go to hell."

Lisa reached out and found Lige's hand. The pressure of her grip told Lige more than any words.

"Go to hell," Lige roared and dropped to the floor. He knew what the answer to that would be.

"Stay close to the base of the wall," he said in a low voice. This house offered good protection, as it was built of hand-hewn logs, chinked with clay. Only the chinking and the windows would be vulnerable.

The answer came in a barrage of rifle fire. The rifle reports pounded at Lige's ears. This was rough enough on a man. His rage rose as he thought what it must be doing to Lisa.

A window glass shattered, and bullets screamed across the room to lodge in the logs of the opposite wall. Their impact made a sharp, distinct sound like the slap of an open hand. An occasional slug chewed away a piece of the chinking, the particles dropping to the floor.

Lige flattened himself against the floor, trying to make himself smaller. He never let go of Lisa's hand, and he was aware of the power in that small hand's grip.

Lige worried that Lisa might become hysterical from terror, then he saw how far wrong that reasoning was, for she said clearly, "I'm getting madder and madder, Lige."

He wanted to laugh in relief, and instead he said, "You'll do."

Lige felt they were safe for the time being, for this bombardment was relatively harmless unless a bullet ricocheted across the room, striking one of them, but that would be unlikely. Lige shook his head and changed his thinking. A man could drive himself crazy worrying about possibilities.

"You all right, Lisa?" he asked during a lull in the firing.

"I could kill every one of them," she said passionately. "Lige, they're shooting the hell out of my home."

Lige wanted to grin. It would take more than terror to dampen her spirit. "All they're doing is wasting a lot of ammunition," he said. He cocked his head, listening. He hadn't heard a shot for a long spell now. "Sounds like they're beginning to realize that."

He peered out of the corner of a window again. He ducked at the flash of flame, and the bullet hit the wall behind him. He had been a little too quick in his prediction.

He looked out of the window again, cautiously easing the rifle barrel out ahead of him. He remembered where that flash came from, and he searched in that direction, seeking something that looked out of place. Ah, he thought, as he squinted down the barrel. That might be just a natural hump in the ground, or it could be a man who had crawled closer. His breathing quickened as he thought he detected movement. He had no way of being sure, but it was worth a shot. He squeezed the trigger, and his teeth bared in wicked satisfaction as he heard a scream. The scream rose higher and higher, then died abruptly in mid-note. Lige thought he could safely say one of the skulking bastards had been hit.

"Did you get one of them?" Denvers asked from across the room. He was at a rear wall, trying to keep an eye open for an attack that could come from that direction.

"I think so," Lige replied. "Stay down," he warned. "They'll open up again."

The words were hardly out of his mouth when the new fusillade came. If anything it was greater in volume than the first one. Somebody out there was damned mad.

Wirt Thomas crawled over to Inman and said tight-lipped, "We're not doing any good, boss."

Inman nodded reluctantly. He had come to the same conclusion, but in his rage at seeing one of his men cut down he had fired in furious abandonment. "He got Barnes, didn't he?"

"Yes."

Inman looked over to where the dark figure lay. "I heard him scream," he said flatly. "How bad is he?"

"I haven't tried to crawl out there to see," Thomas replied. He broke into furious swearing. "We wasted a hell of a lot of ammunition. With one shot, they get Barnes." His face twisted with the sense of loss. "I tried to warn him he was trying to get too close, but he was so goddamned eager to get Lige." He turned his face from Inman to hide the emotion there. "Haze Barnes was my best friend," he said brokenly.

Inman shook his head in sympathy. "I know. You and Haze hired on at the same time. Do you think he's dead?"

"I know he is," Thomas said savagely. "He hasn't moved. Oh God, if there was some way we could flush out that bastard."

"There might be," Inman said slowly. "If we could set fire to that house."

"How do you suggest we do that?" Thomas snarled. He was wild with frustration. "Just walk up and touch a match to it?"

"Easy, Wirt," Inman said soothingly. "I'm not suggesting anything that foolish. But that roof is wood shingles. If a man could ride up and toss a torch up there, those shingles would burn, wouldn't they?"

The wildness was lessening in Thomas. "You always had a head," he said admiringly. "What are you going to make that torch out of that the wind won't whip out? A rider sure ain't going to be able to take it slow."

"A good pine knot wouldn't go out," Inman said. "Once it's started, it's hard to blow out."

"I want to carry that torch," Thomas said.

Inman looked at him calculatingly. "I thought you would," he murmured.

It had been a long, nerve-wracking silence, and Lisa broke it by asking, "Do you think they've given up, Lige?"

"Not them," Lige said decisively. "They're just figuring out some other way to get at us."

Lige peered out into the darkness again, remembering telling Lisa that all that was on his mind was to get through the night. He thought with sorrowful humor he hadn't planned on a night this long.

His eyes sharpened as he saw the dark blob of motion. The pound of horse hoofs was clearly audible before Lige could see the running animal. He stared hard, trying to make out what the rider carried. It looked like a small ball of fire that moved as the horse came on.

"Get away from here, Lisa," he commanded sharply. "It's coming again." Now he realized what the rider carried. It was some kind of a torch. It would be ineffectual against the logs of the wall, but those shingles were vulnerable. He sucked in a breath as he thought of what that torch could do, if it landed on the roof.

Lisa had scarcely moved away when the covering fire for the rider broke out. Lige ignored the danger, staying where he was. He had to stop that rider before he reached tossing distance with that torch.

He flinched as a bullet ripped through the window, but he never took his eyes off the oncoming rider. That bullet was much closer than he liked. God, how he wanted to squeeze the trigger. Still, he forced himself to wait. A running target was difficult at best, and one coming straight on was the hardest shot of all. Lige wanted to empty the rifle, but wild, hasty shooting would accomplish nothing but wasted ammunition.

The rider was within sixty yards of the house. Lige could plainly see the flaming torch he carried aloft. It could be only a figment of his imagination, but Lige thought he could make out the narrowed eyes, the contorted face of the rider who carried the torch. Lige squeezed the trigger, and his lips grew tighter as he knew he had missed. The rider was still secure in the saddle. Lige pumped in another shell and fired again.

The rider reared straight in the stirrups, then slowly began to bend. He attempted to straighten and throw the torch before he slid from the horse, but it was a feeble effort. The torch landed harmlessly some twenty-five yards from the house. The riderless horse whirled and galloped away.

Lige felt only a hollow where his stomach should have been, and moisture trickled down his face. The dead rider lay about thirty yards from the house, and a few yards ahead of him the torch still burned.

Lige raised a hand and wiped the sweat from his face. Lisa started to move toward him, and he snapped, "Stay there, Lisa. They'll open up again."

It took no prophet to forecast that. After another failure, whoever was out there would be driven wild by frustration.

Lige flattened against the base of the wall as bullets ripped through the windows. He could hear some of them sinking into the logs outside.

As the firing died, Lisa crawled over to where Lige lay.

"At that rate they should be just about out of ammunition," he said wryly.

He anticipated the question on her face and shook his head. "No, it isn't over, Lisa. That rider got pretty close. It'll encourage them to try again." He knew what he would do, if he were in their boots. He wouldn't send a single rider; he would send all he had. The few defenders in the house couldn't protect themselves against a concentrated rush.

He had to say something, and his tongue was suddenly clumsy. "Lisa, I want you to know something. If things turn out wrong, I want you to know—"

She pressed her fingers against his lips. "Do you think you have to tell me?" she whispered. "I've known ever since the day you protected me at the stage."

She removed her fingers and kissed him. The kiss was light and brief, but it told him everything.

"Lisa," he faltered, and tears stung his eyes.

"We'll talk about it later," she said.

Lige wished he could believe there would be a later.

Inman went into an insane fury as he saw Thomas fall. "Goddamn them," he raved. "They got Wirt." He fought off the terrible impulse to jump to his feet and rush that house.

He forced himself to think more clearly. They had been so close to success when Thomas went down. He looked at Hamp, and there was a stealthy speculation in his eyes. "Thomas almost got there. A lucky shot got him. It won't happen again."

Hamp squirmed uneasily under the intensity of Inman's scrutiny. "What are you trying to say?" he mumbled.

"I've lost two damned good men. I've listened to you long enough saying how much you want Lige. Now you can prove it."

Hamp's mouth sagged open as he got Inman's meaning. "You saying you want me to make that crazy ride." He shook his head, a dogged, determined gesture. "I've seen them prove twice just how good shots they are."

"Are you saying you're a lesser man than Wirt?" Inman sneered.

"I don't want any comparison with him at all," Hamp said stubbornly. "He's dead."

"I never thought I'd see a Matlock show chicken liver," Inman said contemptuously.

"That's enough," Travis said.

Inman glared at Travis and opened his mouth.

"I said that's enough," Travis snapped.

Inman couldn't meet those fierce eyes. "Do you want to give up?" he blustered.

"I'm not saying anything like that," Travis said coldly. "But if you want Lige so much, why don't you go in after him?"

Inman was hemmed in by three Matlocks. He wanted to smash at all of them, but he couldn't handle all three.

"If anybody's going in, everybody's going," Travis said flatly. "But you're not picking one of my boys to be your cat's-paw."

Inman still glowered, but what Travis said diverted his thoughts along a new line. If they all advanced together, they could disperse the defenders' fire. Inman would bet that one of them would get close enough to the house to toss a torch onto the roof. His throat tightened as he thought, which one?

"Make up your mind," Travis said. "Do we go, or do we give up?"

"It might work at that," Inman muttered. "Each one will go in on a different angle. They can't shoot fast enough to stop all of us."

"Let's be at it," Travis said grimly. "We'll need four more pine knots."

Hamp and Ordie nodded, but there wasn't much enthusiasm in them. They had seen evidence of Lige's ability with a rifle. This had turned out to be far more deadly than either of them expected. From the start this hadn't been a simple matter of calling Lige out, then gunning him down.

Inman found a pine knot bigger than his doubled fists, but the limb was too large to hold in one hand.

"I've got to whittle down a handle," he said. His throat was dry, and a cold wind played up and down his spine. He knew with a certainty that one or more of them wouldn't reach the house. That depended upon how fast and accurate the return fire was. The thought kept slugging away at Inman's mind.

He pulled a knife from his pocket, and Travis watched him suspiciously. "Sure, you ain't stalling, Harley?"

Inman flushed. "What the hell do you mean by that?"

"It seems to me you ain't exactly burning up to get on with this."

The words impugned Inman's courage, and he bristled. "I didn't see any of you jumping up to take Barnes' or Thomas's place," he said hotly.

Travis ignored what Inman said. "You can go or stay. I don't give a damn. But after what Lige tried to do to Hamp, I can't give up until I even the score." His burning eyes challenged Inman. "We can take care of it without you. But you were the one who made so much talk about getting Lige."

Inman felt the heat in his face. He had lost his hold over Travis. Until now, Travis had never dared to question his orders.

"Come on," Inman snapped. "Let's get mounted."

He had a foot in the stirrup and was ready to swing up when the moon appeared, lighting up the earth.

Inman grabbed at a new excuse for delay. "That moon is going to make it a lot harder," he said.

Travis shrugged without reply and mounted.

The stubborn old fool, Inman raved inwardly. Nothing was going to turn Travis. The icy wind along Inman's spine seemed to increase in volume.

Inman tried to reassume his position of leadership. "We stay together until I give the sign," he said. "Then we'll split. We'll start our run a couple of hundred yards from the house."

Travis looked moodily at him and didn't speak. Inman cursed him inwardly. This was the last time he would have anything to do with a Matlock. After tonight he was through with them.

Inman waited until the torches were lit. "Ready?" he asked and lifted the reins. He let the reins fall back and cocked his head.

"Now what's holding you up?" Travis asked acidly.

"I heard something," Inman muttered. "Listen!"

"I don't hear a damned thing," Travis said flatly. "Why in the hell don't you just drop out? It'd make all of us happier." His face was suffused with passion as he sought for further words. His expression changed all of a sudden, and the passion was gone.

"I do hear something," he admitted. He listened a moment longer, then said frozenly, "I hear horses." His head swiveled about as he tried to pick up the source of the sound.

"There," he cried. "To the right of the house! Six horses, coming like hell."

Inman had seen them, too. Six riders coming, as Travis said, like hell. Inman felt more relief than frustration. He couldn't identify any of the riders at this distance, but he had a feeling one of them was Duncan.

Travis confirmed Inman's guess. "That's Duncan," he said dully. His shoulders sagged, and his face fell into ruin. Duncan's arrival meant help for Lige.

"I guess our plans are no good now." Travis sighed and turned his horse away from the house. "There'll be another night."

Inman hadn't moved. "Take Hamp home with you," he said spitefully. "He started everything by trying to rob a dead sheepherder's pockets. I don't want to be around him any more."

Inman sank his spurs viciously into his horse's flanks and galloped away.

Travis stared after him, then shook his head. "That miserable bastard. I've done too much listening to him. Come on, boys."

"What are we going to do now?" Hamp wailed.

"Stop that bellyaching," Travis said in disgust. "We're going home. If anybody asks any questions, we haven't stirred from the house all night." His rage still burned at Lige. Inman was wrong when he said Hamp had started all of the trouble in the first place. It was all Lige's doing.

CHAPTER TWENTY-THREE

It's been too quiet, Lige thought, and his worry increased. Surely, he should have heard at least one shot. But there was only darkness and silence out there, and both had equal pressure. He felt like yelling with jubilation as the moon appeared, highlighting objects that had been obscured before. He saw one man lying fairly near the house, and he could pick out the body of the first one he shot. The moonlight was a godsend. It should enable him to shoot more accurately.

"See anything, Cleve?" Lige called across the room.

"Not a damned thing," Denvers replied. "This silence is worse than the shooting."

Lige smiled at Lisa, who had stayed close to him. Neither of them had spoken very much, but they didn't need words to strengthen the feeling each knew existed in the other.

"Maybe they've gone away," Lisa said hopefully.

"Sure," Lige agreed. He didn't believe that at all, but he could see no percentage in increasing her worry. He glanced out of the window and stiffened. Lisa's hope was being shattered, for Lige counted six riders out there.

His heart began to pound. This was the way he would have handled the situation if he wanted to dig somebody out of this house. Those men out there knew or could guess how many defenders were in this house. A concentrated attack was bound to overrun them.

His eyes narrowed as he watched the riders. What were they doing now? They had stopped in a fairly tight group. Probably talking over their plans, he thought. His rifle's range could reach them, but that would do more harm than good. A shot would only scatter them, giving them a chance to regroup.

"Cleve," he said, "come over here. A bunch of riders off to the left of this window."

Lige didn't look at Lisa. He couldn't bear to see the hope die on her face.

Before Denvers reached him, a voice yelled, "Lige, do you hear me?"

Lige went all loose and limp inside. Sure, he knew that voice, but at the moment, his relief was so great he couldn't speak.

"Damn it, Lige," the voice roared impatiently, "it's Cass. Answer me."

"Come in, Cass," Lige yelled at the top of his voice.

Now, Lige could look at Lisa. "It's over," he said simply.

Lisa wanted to rush into his arms, and Lige wanted to hold her, but Denvers was there.

Lige grinned at her and moved to the door. He flung it wide and stepped outside. The pounding of those hoofs coming toward him was the most pleasant sound he would ever hear.

Duncan pulled up before him. "Didn't want you shooting my head off," he grumbled.

"I would have tried," Lige said. "My God, Cass, I can't tell you how glad I am to see you."

Duncan looked at the bullet-pocked walls of the house. "I can imagine," he said drily.

Lige shook his head in wonder. "You picked the right time."

"Not me," Duncan disclaimed. "Andy rode into town and told me he thought Travis was going after you. I thought I'd better look into it."

Lige walked over to where Brunner sat. He rested a hand on Brunner's knee and said, "I owe you, Andy." For the first time, he noticed Brunner's battered face. "Good God, Andy. What happened to you?"

"Travis." Brunner shook his head at the question forming on Lige's face. "Drop it, Lige. It's my own business." His eyes hardened. "No man kicks me in the face and gets away with it."

"Andy, I'm sorry," Lige said. He hated to see the old bond between Travis and Brunner broken. It had to be something drastic to shatter it so thoroughly. Lige didn't care what the reason was. He was just grateful it had sent Brunner after Duncan.

"Get down, Andy," Lige said. "Your face needs attention."

Brunner protested, but at Lige's insistence he swung down. The effort made him breathe hard, and there was distress in the sound. Brunner must be hurting bad.

"Be right back," Lige said to Duncan and went inside with Brunner.

"Lisa, this is Andy Brunner," Lige said. "We owe him a lot. He brought Duncan here."

"I'm grateful," she said softly to Brunner. "Oh, your face," she cried in concern.

"Do what you can for him, Lisa," Lige said. He didn't try to explain anything to her. Brunner wouldn't appreciate any talk about the way he looked. "I'll be back soon."

Lige joined Duncan outside. Duncan was studying the bullet damage to the walls and windows. "They hit you pretty hard," he observed.

"They got every window in the place," Lige grunted. "You should see the inside."

"Got any idea who they were?" Duncan asked.

"I know," Lige replied.

"Good," Duncan said with satisfaction. "Then you got a good look at them?"

His satisfaction faded at Lige's shaking head.

"I heard them, Cass. It's just as good as seeing them." At the doubt spreading across Duncan's face, he said heatedly, "I heard Inman and Hamp. Both of them called out that if I stepped outside, they'd leave the others alone." He grinned bleakly. "Denvers and Lisa had a different view. Do you think I wouldn't know those voices?"

Duncan's doubt was dispelled. "No," he said.

"I got a couple of them. One is over there." Lige jerked a thumb toward where the body lay.

"I saw him on the way in," Duncan said. "Know him?"

"I never got that close, Cass."

"Let's go see who he is," Duncan said.

Duncan swung down from his horse, and as they walked together, Lige said, "He came at us riding like a crazy Indian. He was carrying a torch. I think he hoped to toss it on the roof. I didn't give him time to tell me what he wanted. I dropped him."

Duncan looked contemplatively at the body. "Good thing you did. Burning you out would have made things a hell of a lot easier for them."

"It sure would," Lige said gravely.

They reached the body, and Duncan toed it over. By the stamp of agony on Thomas's face he had died hard.

"Thomas," Duncan said flatly. "He wouldn't be here on his own. It had to be Inman's doing. I want to see the other one."

He stood for a long moment, staring down at Barnes. "Haze Barnes," he said in that same musing tone. Duncan looked back at the house. "Pretty good shot," he commented. He slammed a fist into his palm. "I'd like to hear Inman talk his way out of this."

As they walked back toward the house, Duncan said, "I was kinda hoping the second one would be Hamp. It would save a headache all around."

Lige's nod was answer enough. "He'll be running hard by now, Cass."

"Probably," Duncan grunted.

"I've got to go in and see how Andy's coming along," Lige said. "Want to come in?"

Duncan shook his head. "I'll wait out here."

Lisa had relit the lamp, and Lige stared about him. The place was a shambles. Broken glass was everywhere on the floor, and there wasn't an item of furniture that didn't have its bullet hole or gouge.

"Look at this," Lisa wailed. "Most of my dishes are shattered. Lige, I'll never get this place back in order."

He wanted to tell her how lucky they were to have come through this untouched, but he held his tongue. Right now, she didn't feel so lucky.

Denvers was there, but Brunner was gone.

"Where did Andy go?" Lige demanded sharply.

Lige thought Lisa was going to cry with frustration. "He wouldn't let me do much for him, Lige. The minute you were gone, he said there was something he had to do. Before I could even reason with him, he slipped out of the door."

"Oh God," Lige groaned. It wasn't hard to figure where Brunner had gone. Lige remembered that ruined face and the blaze in Brunner's eyes. Andy was a prideful man. Lige didn't know the cause of the argument between Brunner and Travis, but he knew Andy would never let it lie where it was.

"I'll be back as soon as I can, Lisa," he said and hurried out of the door. She called something after him that he didn't fully catch, and he shook his head. He didn't have time to wait for an explanation.

He rushed over to Duncan and said, "Andy took off the minute you and I got out of sight, Cass."

Duncan studied Lige intently. "You've got a good idea where he went?"

"I have," Lige said, tight-lipped. He cut Duncan off short before Duncan offered to go with him. "I want to handle this myself, Cass."

Duncan swore in exasperation, then broke off as the unrelenting set of Lige's face didn't change.

"I hope you know what you're doing," he said and sighed.

"I hope so too, Cass. Do you want me to bring them back here?"

Duncan scowled and pulled at his lower lip. Lige hadn't said it, but Duncan knew what he meant. Should he bring back any survivors?

"Might as well," Duncan said. "I'll go over and pick up

Inman. This is as good a place to meet as any. Sure you don't want me to go along?"

Lige didn't miss the pleading in Duncan's voice. "Something I've got to handle, Cass. Can I take one of your men's horses? He can take mine. It's in the shed. I haven't time to saddle him."

"Sure," Duncan said gruffly. "Good luck, Lige."

Lige mounted the borrowed horse. He looked down at Duncan and said, "Thanks, Cass." He whipped the horse around in the direction of Travis's house. Oh, damn it. Why had Brunner been so hardheaded? Why hadn't he waited for Lige to join him? Lige kicked the horse into a faster pace. He didn't know how far behind he was. He kicked the horse again as a sense of urgency threatened to overwhelm him.

CHAPTER TWENTY-FOUR

Brunner slowed as he came in view of Travis's house. A light was on in the kitchen. That should mean Travis was home, and Brunner was grateful for that. His head ached unbearably, and the rage within him hurt almost as much as his face. He didn't want to have to go searching half of the night for Travis.

Brunner dismounted a hundred yards from the house and approached the kitchen window on foot. He looked through the window and saw Travis and Ordie were there. Travis sat in a chair, and Ordie paced restlessly. Brunner had never seen Travis look so old and beaten. Travis's hands dangled between his knees, and he looked as though he didn't have strength to raise them.

Brunner moved to the door, seized the knob, and flung the door wide. One long step carried him inside. The noise of his entrance whipped both heads toward him. Ordie's mouth was half open, and Travis looked stunned.

Brunner cursed Travis in low, passionate tones. "Nobody does what you did to me, Travis, without paying," he finished. "Get up."

Travis shrank before the unbridled fury in Brunner's eyes. "Hold it, Andy," he pleaded. "You don't know what I was going through." His voice was hoarse and cracked. "Andy, I wish it hadn't happened."

"No good," Brunner said, shaking his head. His hand hovered over his gun butt. "You can just sit there, or get up and try to defend yourself."

Travis's face was ashen as he read the implacable determination in Brunner's face. Once, Brunner had been frighteningly good with that gun. Did some of that ability still remain?

"He ain't getting up," Hamp said, stepping into the room. He held a gun, and his face was set with wicked purpose.

Brunner's face went tight from the surprise of Hamp's unexpected appearance. He knew he wasn't going to pay Travis back.

"Damn you, Hamp," he choked, and a crippled hand tried to find some of its old speed.

"You never were very bright, Andy," Hamp said, as he shot Brunner.

Brunner's crippled fingers never reached his gun. His face went rigid with shock as the bullet slammed into his chest. He fought to stay erect, but all of the strength was gone from his bones. He collapsed suddenly and pitched forward on his face.

"Now, you've done it," Travis said in dull stupefaction.

"What did you want me to do?" Hamp snarled at him. "Let him shoot you?" He shrugged those heavy shoulders. "I ain't any worse off than I was."

"Maybe you ain't," Travis said bitterly. "But how about Ordie and me?"

Lige heard the shot just as he reached Brunner's horse. For the past few seconds, he had been wondering why Andy left his horse here, then had realized Brunner didn't want the sound of hoofs to alert Travis. Lige was too late and knew it, and the knowledge made him sick to his stomach.

He spurred the horse regardless of the noise it might make. He jumped off and crossed the porch. The door was open. Travis and Hamp were engaged in a violent quarrel, and the noise of Lige's horse hadn't gotten through to them.

Hamp stood a few feet from Brunner's body, his gun still in his hand. Some instinct told Lige he could do nothing for Andy. Andy was dead.

Lige drew and stepped through the doorway. "Drop the gun, Hamp," he said, his voice as brittle as thin ice. He heard the hard rasp of Hamp's breath. Hamp was turned from Lige, and he tried to whirl.

"Don't try it," Lige yelled.

If Hamp heard the order, it didn't register. His eyes were wild in a tight pinched face, and his lips were pulled back, baring his teeth. He finished his turn and tried to whip up the gun he held.

Lige shot him once. Hamp looked as though he was falling apart, but he still remained on his feet. Some bull-like vitality held him erect, and he hadn't dropped his gun, though its weight must be tremendous by the effort he used trying to raise it.

"Why, damn you," he whispered, and a streak of blood stained his face from mouth to chin.

Lige shot him again. The first shot was for Pancho; the second for Brunner.

Lige whipped around to face Travis and Ordie before Hamp fell. He heard the thud of Hamp's body as it struck the floor but didn't look around.

"You killed Hamp," Travis said in shocked horror. He seemed incapable of rising. Ordie stood there, looking stupid and foolish at the sudden turn of events.

Ordie wore his gun, and Lige said levelly, "If you've got any fool idea of trying to use that thing, Ordie, you're out of your mind. You'd better tell him, Travis, or you won't have a son left."

The harsh words shocked Travis back to reality. "Don't try it, Ordie," he begged. "He means it."

Ordie carefully moved his hand away from his gun, and the wildness faded from his eyes. He licked his lips and didn't say anything.

"Lige, you can't blame us for Andy," Travis begged. "Hamp shot Andy."

"I know," Lige said tersely. "Take off those gun belts. Careful," he warned.

The hate was back in Ordie's eyes, but he wasn't insane enough to disobey Lige's command. He unbuckled the gun belt and let it drop to the floor.

Lige motioned with his gun. "I mean it, Travis," he said quietly.

Travis stood, an old, beaten man. He unbuckled his gun belt and let it fall. "My God, Lige," he whispered, "what are you going to do?"

"Take you back to Duncan," Lige replied. "He's at Denvers' place. He'll take over there."

Travis's face looked like a rain-soaked mass of dough. "You'd do that," he whimpered, "after all I did for you?"

Lige was sickened with the loathing he felt. "Move," he snapped. "Go out and get on your horses. I'd just as soon shoot both of you right now."

Travis and Ordie stumbled out of the door ahead of Lige. They were beaten men, and Lige knew it. He wouldn't have the slightest trouble with either of them.

They rode before him, sitting slackly in their saddles. Just the same Lige was relieved to see a group of men before Denvers' house. Duncan had made a quick trip after Inman.

Duncan looked at Travis and Ordie and asked sardonically, "What took you so long?"

"Just fooling around I guess, Cass." Lige's voice hardened. "Hamp's dead. He wouldn't listen to me. He shot Andy before I got there."

"Ah," Duncan said. The single word showed his distress. "I guess it's all wrapped up, Lige. Inman's over there." He jerked his head toward Inman, standing against the wall. Inman had the same beaten look that Travis and Ordie had.

"Come on, Harley," Duncan said. "Back on your horse. We're ready to go now."

"What are you going to do to me?" Inman asked. The old bravado was gone, leaving his voice a mere squeak.

"That's up to Judge Hacker," Duncan replied. He grinned wolfishly at Inman. "I'd say he's got a lot to hold you three on. At the very least, I'll bet you're gonna pay a chunk to make up for the damage you've caused."

Inman rocked his head from side to side, his face stricken. "God," he bleated. "That could break me."

"I'm hurting for you," Duncan said, his grin broadening. "Move. I won't tell you again."

Duncan mounted and looked down at Lige. "Let me know if you manage to stir up any more trouble."

"Cass, I sure will," Lige said fervently. "Does this end the trouble?"

"I'd say for a while," Duncan said soberly. "What happens to these three will be an object lesson that will put a damper on others who might come up with similar crazy ideas. It'll keep a rein on them for a long time, maybe for years." He shook his head in reflection. "You can't bet on this, but some times men learn something. Maybe this is one of them."

He nodded to Lige and lifted his reins.

Lige watched the group ride away. He heard Lisa come up beside him, but for a moment didn't look at her. He wanted to savor the anticipation of seeing the old radiance return to her face.

"Lige, it's all over, isn't it?" Lisa asked in a small voice.

Lige remembered what Duncan had just said, as he turned to face her. "It looks like it, Lisa. At least, for a while."

"What are you going to do now?" Lisa asked. Her eyes searched his face, trying to read an answer there before he spoke.

"I kinda got used to sheep," Lige said thoughtfully. "Guess I'll stick around."

"Oh Lige," she said, and came into his arms.

Denvers was watching all this, but Lige didn't care. He kissed Lisa. His anticipation didn't nearly prepare him for the promise in her lips.

Lige raised his head and looked at Denvers. His eyes were challenging.

"I figured something like this was bound to happen," Denvers grumbled. He shook his head and, for a moment, Lige thought there was displeasure in the gesture. "You're going into a bad business," Denvers said gruffly. "You've seen what can happen."

Duncan's words still rang in Lige's mind. "Maybe it won't happen again, Cleve. You can't talk me out of it."

"I guess not," Denvers said thoughtfully. "Lisa—"

Denvers hesitated, and Lige knew a stab of alarm. Denvers wasn't through with his objections.

"Lisa, I can't send you back to school next fall," Denvers said. "With all the losses I've had, I can't afford it."

Lige wanted to point out that Denvers was worrying unnecessarily. If the court decided against Travis and Inman, all of Denvers' losses would be made up. Prudence held back Lige's words. Denvers had heard what Duncan said; he knew all this.

"Guess a man has to get used to changes," Denvers said. "It's been a long night. I'm going to bed." He nodded to them and walked into the house.

"Poor Pa," Lisa said. "There goes his biggest dream."

Lige pulled her back to him. "Maybe you're wrong, Lisa. He's a smart old boy. I think he's just changed his dream."

"Yes," Lisa breathed before she lifted her lips to him.